[*Frontispiece.*

ANCIENT AND HOLY WELLS

OF

CORNWALL

BY

M. AND L. QUILLER-COUCH

LONDON

CHAS. J. CLARK

4 LINCOLN'S INN FIELDS, W.C.

1894

First published 1894
This edition 1994

Tamara Publications
60 Culverland Park
Liskeard
Cornwall PL14 3HY

British Library Cataloguing in Publication Data
CIP data for this book is available from the British Library

ISBN 0 9512822 5 5

Printed in Great Britain by
Latimer Trend & Company Ltd, Plymouth

INTRODUCTION.

Every now and then there issues a vein of writing, like a spring of natural water, which is pure gold. This unique and exquisite volume was written a century ago by Mabel and Lillian Quiller-Couch using their father's notes.

They were the daughters of Thomas Quiller-Couch, a doctor who practised in Bodmin and lived at 63 Fore Street, until his death in 1884. He was a kindly and gifted physician who, when treating the poor of those harsh Victorian days, was apt to charge little or nothing, and died bequeathing a meagre inheritance to his children.

Their grandfather, Sir Jonathan Couch, had also practised medicine in the picturesque village of Polperro, produced a notable book on the scientific study of fish. It was he who wrote what was, in those far-off days, a standard four-volume work, *The History of British Fishes*, as well as a *History of Polperro*.

Lillian married a don of English at London University, John Hay Lobban, and settled in Hampstead. Mabel, who never married, joined her. It was to his brother-in-law that Sir Arthur Quiller-Couch, so familiar to students of English Literature as "Q", dedicated *On the Art of Writing*.

Many subsequent writers, particularly J. Meyrick's *A Pilgrim's Guide to The Holy Wells of Cornwall* has very valuable map references, along with Paul Broadhurst's *Secret Shrines*, which has some beautiful photographs, owe an immense debt of historical and literary gratitude to Dr. Thomas Quiller-Couch and his daughters, Mabel and Lillian, whose work here is faithfully reproduced.

Their simple style and detailed research deserve a wider following. Their inimitable language merits a far higher place than posterity has, thus far, awarded them—especially in this age when so much of our native heritage and culture has been lost or destroyed.

Indeed, when Dr. Thomas Quiller-Couch somewhat sadly noted, "Hydromancy is dead in this generation", he little knew what he had started! We, his beneficiaries, have this matchless volume with which to honour their memories and resurrect that peerless past of those truly Cornish days when the well was the font and fount of village life. These wells were gifted with supernatural properties and were thought to have powers of healing, dispensation, divination and other privileges of exceptional peculiarity dating from Druidic times, in what was to become "The Land of The Saints".

PETER MOORE. 1994

Dedication

Aunt Susan

This reprint is for my aunt, Susan.
A great country-lover who appreciates
such things.

CONTENTS.

LIST OF ILLUSTRATIONS.

PREFACE.

On turning over a book of manuscript notes on the ancient and holy wells of Cornwall, which had been collected from time to time by the late Mr. Thomas Quiller-Couch, we considered that these same notes might be arranged, the present condition of the wells therein mentioned ascertained, and some account given of any others of which we could find any trace. This idea has been most faithfully carried out, to the best of our ability; but the number of wells, which amounted to about forty in the original MS., swelled to more than ninety before the list was completed. A "pilgrimage" of several months' duration has been made to these sacred springs; therefore, in most cases the following account of their condition may be relied on as being that of an eye-witness, though, unfortunately, tidings of some holy wells reached us after we had left the county and were unable to revisit it. Even now we fear that there may be some which have received no notice whatever: if this be the case, the omission arises from ignorance of their existence, not from any desire to pass them over. It is difficult, even now, to gain authentic information of the old customs, ceremonies, and traditions of these holy springs, so quickly and surely does the hand of civilisation and progress wipe away the old beliefs and superstitions. That superstition still lingers among the Cornish is beyond doubt; but it lurks in their minds, and betrays itself in the wearing of a secret charm, or the half-playful dropping of a pin into the well by the sentimental maiden; not in serious visitations to the consecrated spot, with solemn ceremonies, in search of health or tidings of the future, as in former times.

A history of the ancient and holy wells of Cornwall had been a favourite idea with Mr. Quiller-Couch for many years before his death, and most of his scanty leisure time was spent in visiting them and collecting information on the subject. During his last illness it was understood that a rough sketch of the preface was being written; whether this was the case or not, nothing but the few following notes on loose scraps of paper has ever been found. It has been thought best to give them as they are, without any attempt to work them into complete form.

"I have for many years been thinking of a booklet about the holy wells of Cornwall; have made many, not painful, pilgrimages to them, with my wallet, pen, and pencil, and gathered many notes of a class of antiquities fast being swept away. . . . The following pages on the holy wells of Cornwall are the result of much pleasant research in deep glens, green lanes, by pleasant villages, farms, and church hamlets; on bare bleak hills where water was little to be looked for, or nestling by some cliff where the salt sea spray sometimes invaded it. In places the most remote and secluded, the old pisky tutelage of prehistoric date still clings to and protects them, and still claims to dispense the virtues of the water. In others the presiding fairy, if consulted in due season and with proper ceremony, will give prophecy of the future. Some springs have the power,—if the presiding spirit has the power, on being appealed to by ceremonies right, and appropriate gifts,—of giving [dispensation] from special troubles (from hanging); special privileges [are gained by those who drink from the well of] St. Keyne.

"The spirit of the well, this naiad, is with us not easily moved to anger, but can be revengeful. These water spirits are, however, generally pacific and aidful, *e.g.*, that of St. Cleer. . . .

"Being, of necessity, a very desultory antiquary, my studies more among men than books, I have set down my notes on a special class of our national antiquities,—a fast-decaying class, which my wanderings within narrow bounds have brought me acquainted with. The history of the holy wells of Cornwall, their structures as still standing, and the remains of well-worship still to be observed or to be picked up from the 'superstitious idle-headed eld' living near them, has been one of the subjects which has relieved me at intervals from other very urgent pursuits. I am very thankful that my natural inclination and early training have compensated for the narrowness of my range, by blessing me with an eye to mark and a heart to enjoy such things as lie within it.

"The saints' wells of my county and their legendary history have been pet joys of mine, and many a pleasant pilgrimage have I made to them, —sweet journeys through lanes of flower and fern and moss, sweet villages and farms, the air as redolent of health as the waters I was in search of. Sometimes over-barren, inasmuch as the delvings of miner, navvy, and quarryman have drained the fountain, and driven [from it] naiad, and saint, and peasant. Two I especially mention: the Holy Well of St. Breward, and St. Cyr's Well of Luxulyan,[1] now falling fast to the ground. The first will soon only exist in a sketch I made some twenty years ago,[2] and the engraving from it in Blight's *Crosses, etc., of East Cornwall;* the second

[1] For present state see p. 58. [2] See p. 17.

in a few sketches and my records. I have been instrumental in re-edifying more than one, and in inciting to the preservation of several more. . . . In another generation the structures will have fallen, the 'fair humanities of old religion' and their ceremonies, now only lingering in the memories of hoary-headed eld, will have gone for ever.

"The date of these rites is buried in the remotest past, in the age before records; and our speculations about it are of necessity vague and unsatisfying. Each individual observer offers in his turn his theory drawn from the buried past. The geologist is satisfied with his researches as proof of the earlier existence of our race than that generally accepted; he gives us pictures of an age when the paleolithic man walked over fields of ice and snow, and made his prey of the cave bear, the mammoth, and other animals long since extinct. This is fairly deducible from the finding of flint tools fashioned by human hand, fished up from the beds of lakes, or set in stalactitic rock as flies in amber, buried in drift deposits, in intimate company with these relics of a contemporary human race.

"The age of man's appearance on this earth is yet a matter of speculation, but there is evidence enough to show it is much beyond that of popular chronology. This is a matter not unconnected with our present subject, as the hand which fashioned so skilfully the barbed arrow-head of flint and the polished hammer-axes may be fairly associated with a brain of high capabilities, and to have had as an outcome of this capacity a religion of some rude sort, wherein what he observed around him, as the elements, were deified, and rocks and trees, wells and running brooks, had each its indwelling genius, its favour to be courted or anger deprecated. All these considerations of a very large subject are here only touched slightly. The labours of the most learned are rewarded by scanty facts, and their deductions only vaguely probable; the speculations of one person mislead, and the fancies of another, which have here free scope, are unsatisfying.

"My humble aim in this little book is to save, within my very small tether, by pen and pencil, all that continues to us of a nearly extinct faith, its material remains, and its legendary fragments. I fear that if not soon done they will be lost for ever. Within my remembrance the cromlech, the holy well, the way-side cross and inscribed stone, have gone before the utilitarian greed of the farmer and the road man, and the undeserved neglect of that hateful being—the *cui bono* man.

"The pencil and pen can give them less transient remembrance. The old beliefs are fading, as the old temples are decaying; and it is only by seeking out the old folk that any trustworthy accounts of the old well, the legends attached to it, the special virtue of the water, and the rites attending all appeals to it for prophecies of the future, and in sickness, or success in life, can be obtained. Unfortunately for the honest antiquary, many of our fountains have been seized on by the very modern verse writer, who has attached to them the creations of his own fancy,—an offence which I take all opportunity of inveighing against, as little better than the production of a counterfeit medal or the falsification of an historic deed.

"Dr. Borlase, learned, diligent, and excellent antiquary as he was, to whom we are all indebted in an iconoclastic age for having copied for us fair things which time had blurred, seems to have had little sympathy with the faiths of the simple, silly, country folk (I use these adjectives in their older meaning), and to have passed them with something like contempt. At present the oral traditions of a people, their seeming follies even, have become of value as indicating kinship between nations shunted off by circumstances, to use the most modern term, in divergent ways. The community of fable, the remnants of a once widespread faith lingering in ill-adapted fragments, are beginning to be appreciated by the broad historian. The local antiquary who gathers even a fragment is not without his praise.

"T. Q. C."

That springs and wells were worshipped, and that this worship was common to many, if not most, countries, must be accepted as facts; and as the springs and wells were immovable and ever present (for it is only in comparatively modern times that they have been in some cases destroyed) the traces of their sanctity and of the veneration in which they were held are naturally of a more lasting nature than those of the worship of fire and air. Judging from traditions, records, etc., the main history of well-worship may be simply told.

The ancients worshipped the elements; and, doubtless, no proofs need be recorded here to substantiate that fact.[1] Borlase, in his *Antiquities of Cornwall*, has it: "Gildas says that the Druids worshipped mountains and rivers. Nor unlikely; but that they worshipped rocks, stones, and fountains, and imagined them inhabited and actuated by divine intelligences of a lower rank, is still more evident, and may be plainly inferred, not only from their stone monuments, but from the prohibitions of several Gallick councils:"—"Cultores Idolorum, Veneratores Lapidum, accensores Facularum, excolentes sacra Fontium vel Arborum, admonemus ut agnascant quod ipsi se spontanere morti subjiciunt qui Diabolo sacrificare videntur" (Concil.

[1] As far back as the time of Joshua the name En-shemesh, or the Fountain of the Sun, given to a well, indicates the reverence of the ancients for the elements.

Turon., A.D. 567, *Baluz.*, Tom. vi, 1234). And again: "From the several waves and eddies, which the sea, river, or other water exhibited when put into agitation, after a ritual manner, they pretended to foretell with great certainty the event of battles; a way of divining recorded by Plutarch, in his *Life of Cesar*, and still usual among the vulgar in Cornwall, who go to some noted well on particular times of the year, and there observe the bubbles that rise, and the aptness of the water to be troubled, or to remain pure, on their throwing in pins or pebbles, and thence conjecture what shall or shall not befall them. The Druids also (as we have great reason to think) pretended to predict future events, not only from holy wells and running streams, but from the rain and snow water, etc." (p. 140).

In all the phenomena of nature the heathen in Cornwall, as in other parts, saw signs of their gods; and as the sea and rivers had their presiding deities, so the springs and fountains were supposed to be under the guardianship of nymphs who were to be worshipped, propitiated, and adored; these presiding spirits were supposed to possess powers of divination, healing, and inspiring. Ceremonies were performed in all solemnity at the sacred spots, and offerings of goats, lambs, milk, and oil, were made to these naiads.

As time went on and the Christian religion took

hold of the people, saints came from Ireland, and Wales and Brittany, to teach the Cornish folk; and gradually the spring which had been worshipped for its fairy, became consecrated by one of these good and holy men, who had settled near it, and was worshipped for its saint. In some few cases a well still retains its more ancient title of "Fairies' Well," or "Piskies' Well," but in the generality of cases it is called "Holy Well," "Saints' Well," or "Well of St. ——".

The gradual transition from heathen rites to Christian belief and the concessions on either side are simply described in the *Translation of Grimm's Teutonic Mythology*, by Stallybrass,[1] as follows: "Oftentimes the Church . . . either was from the outset, or gradually became, tolerant and indulgent. She prudently permitted, or could not prevent, that heathen and Christian things should here and there run into one another; the clergy themselves would not always succeed in marking off the bounds of the two religions; their private leanings might let some things pass which they found firmly rooted in the multitude. In the language, together with a stock of newly imported Greek and Latin terms, there still remained, even for ecclesiastical use, a number of Teutonic words previously employed in heathen services, just as the names of

[1] Vol. iii, xxxv.

gods stood ineradicable in the days of the week; to such words old customs would still cling, silent and unnoticed, and take a new lease of life. The festivals of a people present a tough material, they are so closely bound up with its habits of life that they will put up with foreign additions if only to save a fragment of festivities long loved and tried. In this way Scandinavia, probably the Goths also for a time, and the Anglo-Saxons down to a late period, retained the heathenish Yule, as all Teutonic Christians did the sanctity of Easter-tide; and from these two the Yule-boar and Yule-bread, the Easter pancake, Easter sword, Easter fire and Easter dance could not be separated. As faithfully were perpetuated the name and, in many cases, the observances of Midsummer. New Christian feasts, especially of saints, seem purposely as well as accidentally to have been made to fall on heathen holidays. Churches often rose precisely where a heathen god or his sacred tree had been pulled down; and the people trod their old paths to the accustomed site: sometimes the very walls of the heathen temple became those of the church; and cases occur in which idol-images still found a place in a wall of the porch, or were set up outside the door, as at Bamberg cathedral there lie Sclavic-heathen figures of animals inscribed with runes. Sacred hills and fountains were re-christened after saints, to whom their sanctity was transferred. . . .

Law-usages, particularly the ordeals and oath-takings, but also the beating of bounds, consecrations, image-processions, spells and formulas, while retaining their heathen character, were simply clothed in Christian forms."

What is true of the Teutonic race may be seen by comparisons to be true of other races in the matter of their gradual transition of religion. The reverence for water was always particularly strong, as being a free gift from some unseen power, bubbling up, or rushing along in an unaccountable manner in the midst of the dry earth. Great was the veneration of the Greeks and Romans for water; with them the bath was entered and quitted with bare head; and votive gifts were placed beside springs and fountains; lambs, milk, and oils were usual offerings, but never wine. In Cornwall, as may be seen in the following pages, there are still a great number of holy wells remaining, and likely to remain for several years to come; though some have suffered greatly from neglect, and others have entirely disappeared. It is curious to note how, in some parts of the county, little trace is left of these small buildings, except a shaped stone or two which may be seen in a farmer's outhouse, or a cottager's garden; while in other parts they are jealously guarded from decay; and again, some springs still have traces of a lingering superstition and veneration, shown in the offerings of pins, which may be seen shining at the bottom of the clear water, and in the visits paid to them for health or divination (generally on Holy Thursday, or some time during May), which superstition has survived the buildings which once stood over them. It is not, as might reasonably be supposed, the spots most largely populated, and nearest to the busy practical world, which are always the least superstitious and most neglectful of their holy wells.

It is also an interesting fact that, with comparatively few exceptions, where there is now a holy well to be seen, either with or without a building to cover it, there are always some remains of a chapel near by also to be seen, or to be heard of in old records; generally the latter, unfortunately, for the chapels of the saints fell into ruin long ago, not one complete building of the sort remaining, though many are the well-buildings yet to be seen standing by the ruins. Many of these wells were doubtless used as baptisteries pertaining to the chapels; but they were also in all probability used by the saints and their followers for domestic purposes; even a saint must drink, and these holy men naturally built their chapels and hermitages near a spring, consecrating the waters, and, in the minds of the simple folk, re-endowing them with rare virtues, which were often real and natural virtues belonging to the waters themselves. To quote Grimm again: "Medical science in heathen times was half-priestly, half-magical. Experience and higher culture gave the priests a knowledge of healing powers in nature; from the sacredness of their office proceeded salutary spells, the use of remedies was backed by sacrifice, nay, great cures and the averting of pestilence could only be effected by sacrifice. Thus all through the Middle Ages we find the Christian priests also possessors, above other men, of medicine and the art of using it."[1] Doubtless in many cases the saints became possessed of the knowledge of the natural virtues of the waters of their consecrated wells, turned it to a good account, and inspired their followers with a deep reverence for these qualities. Wonderful cures were performed at these springs, aided in a great measure, no doubt, by the unquestioning faith of the simple folk.

The Cornish saints, as before mentioned, came mostly from Ireland and Wales; and in these two countries the well-worship carried on, the ceremonies, and superstitions, were almost, if not quite, the same. In Wales, at the present time, it seems that the holy wells are to a great extent neglected, overlooked, and forgotten; the Welsh are by nature a less superstitious people than either the Irish or the Cornish; one is told that here and

[1] Vol. iii, 1150.

there a well may be found with pins, or even coins, left in its waters, or rags tied to the bushes surrounding it, as votive offerings, or a sign of belief in its powers; but there are no shrines over the springs, or very few, and the solemn and regular visits to the consecrated spots on certain holy days are almost unheard of. In Ireland, owing no doubt greatly to the nature of the people and their religion, well-worship, or the customs and ceremonies to which the superstitious cling long after the real worship has been given over, linger to a slightly greater extent, though many and stern attempts have been made from time to time to stamp it out, and the opposition of the Roman Catholic priests to these superstitious practices is banishing them by degrees. "Patterns," *i.e.*, meetings in honour of the patron saint, were very generally held until of late years, but the priests have almost entirely suppressed them. Wells near an old blasted oak or an upright hewn stone, we are told, are most respected (lingering traces of Druidism?), and the visitants will crawl round the wells from east to west on their knees, three, six, or nine times, as a voluntary penance. Of Cornwall's wells the present state may be gathered to some extent from this volume.

In Christian times superstition and belief in the powers of divination, healing, etc., possessed by the waters rose to such a height that well-worship was magisterially interfered with. "The idolatrous adorations of fountains, or of the saints who conferred their virtues, were, in mediæval times, carried to such excess and attended by such gross abuses that well-worship was classed with such crimes as augury, necromancy, etc., and in ecclesiastical canons of the days of Edgar, Canute, and Henry I, was strictly forbidden."—(T. Q. C.) In 1628 several were brought before the Kirk Sessions at Falkirk, accused of going to Christ's well on the Sundays of May "to seek their health," and were sentenced to do penance "in linens three several Sabbaths"; and the people were reminded "that it is statute and ordained" that any persons found after this to have superstitiously and idolatrously passed in pilgrimage to Christ's well to seek their health would be "forced to repent in sacco (sackcloth) and linen three several Sabbaths, pay twenty lib (Scots) toties quoties for ilk fault," or, in default of payment, to be imprisoned on bread and water for "aught days".

The custom of dropping pins into the water, either with a simple wish, or to note by the rising of the bubbles whether good or ill may be expected, is the most general in Cornwall, Ireland, and Wales; the pin is usually bent, probably because crooked things, as a "crooked sixpence," etc., are considered more lucky than others. The custom of tying rags to the surrounding bushes of the spring was only noted at one well in Cornwall, *viz.*, Madron Well, near Penzance,[1] though it is a very general practice in other countries; it is done at curative wells, and from much comparing of statements of this custom in different countries and by different persons, as well as by reasoning the matter, it appears safe to conclude that these rags were not placed there as *offerings*, but—after being touched by the diseased body of the believer—with the hope that the disorder might be communicated to the rag, to disappear from his person as the material decayed, in the same manner as stolen meat, grain, etc., after being used to touch a wart, is supposed to have transferred to it the cause of the complaint, which leaves the body sound and healthy, as the meat or grain rots. At some wells a cross of rushes or straw is floated on the surface of the water, to sink or swim as Fate decides. Coins were also left on a niche in the well, or cast into its waters as an offering; this custom seems to have entirely disappeared in Cornwall at least, although at one well, Jesus Well, St. Minver, it was a distinctly remembered practice: it was probably a much older custom than the dropping in of pins; for setting aside the fact that pins were not in use until the sixteenth century, there is never any mention in the old

[1] See p. 125.

accounts of the skewers of wood or bone of former days being among the offerings to the naiad.

At the curative springs the ceremonies would seem to be even more elaborate and solemn in later years than at those resorted to for divination; the dipping was to take place on a certain day in the year, and at a certain time of the day, in silence, and with certain words of invocation. Three is the most approved number in all these ceremonies; three dips, three walks backward round the well, etc.; and May is the favourite month on the whole, though some waters dispense their particular virtues more freely on Midsummer Day, some on the last day of the year, many at Easter and Ascension Day, and others on Holy Thursday, or on the day sacred to the saint to whom they are dedicated. In France the water which flows from the wells on Easter Day while the church bells ring, is said to possess magical virtues. Prof. Rhys, writing of Manx holy well worship, remarks: "I notice with regard to most of the mountains climbed on the first Sunday of harvest (the 12th of August, if a Sunday, or the first Sunday after the 12th) that they seem to have near their summits wells of some celebrity; and these wells appear to be the goal of the visitor's peregrinations. This is the case with South Barrule, the spring of which cannot, it is said, be found when sought a second time; also with Snaefell and Maughold Head, which boasts one of the most famous springs in the island. When I visited it last summer, in company with Mr. Kermode, we found it to contain a considerable number of pins, some of which were bent, and many buttons. . . . Several people who had resorted many years ago to St. Maughold's Well told me that the water is good for sore eyes, and that after using it on the spot, or filling a bottle with it to take home, one was wont to drop a pin, or bead, or button, into the well. But it had its full virtue only when visited on the first Sunday of harvest, and that only during the hour when the books were open at church, which, shifted back to Roman Catholic times, means doubtless the hour when the priest is engaged saying Mass. This restriction, however, is not peculiar to St. Maughold's Well, as I have heard of it in connection with other wells, such as Chibbyr Lansh in Lezayre parish, and with a well on Sliean Maggyl, in which some Kirk Michael people have a great belief. But even sea water was believed to have considerable virtues if you washed in it while the books were open at church, as I was told by a woman who had many years ago repeatedly taken her own sister to divers wells and to the sea during the service on Sunday, in order to have her eyes cured of their chronic weakness."

The decoration of wells, as in Ireland formerly,

and at Tissington in Derbyshire, and probably several other places, is not heard of in Cornwall.

We do not pretend in this preface and in the following pages to give to the public any learned disquisition on the habits, customs, and religions of the ancients, nor to lay down a hard and fast decision as to how, when, and why these holy wells of Cornwall appeared at all ; we have simply tried to give to these curious little buildings a small volume of their own, telling of their ancient history all that we could glean, and of their present state what we could see ; and these words in preface are humbly placed before the notice of older and more deeply-read antiquaries, as the result of comparisons, criticisms, and amateur reasonings on the subject, after having tried our utmost to sift the grains of truth from the chaff of imaginative and careless writers. The above may seem a simple explanation of the existence of these buildings, but should not be disbelieved on that account—the Cornish were a simple folk, and to a great extent are so still, in the truest and kindest sense of the word ; and if these notes should chance to interest any Cornishman and antiquary, or should be the means of inciting him to the rebuilding or preserving of one of these lingering antiquities—that man will be no worse for them.

Great thanks are due to many friends in Cornwall

and elsewhere, for ready help given and trouble taken, with regard to inquiries concerning these holy wells.

The matter in the following pages having the initials T. Q. C. at the end is from the original MS. as it stands.

ANCIENT AND HOLY WELLS OF CORNWALL.

ST. AGNES WELL.

On the north coast of Cornwall, in a dingle in St. Agnes parish, stood the Well of St. Agnes, near a building once known as Porth Chapel which existed till about the year 1780.

"Age and neglect have done their fell work on the well; and I am indebted, through a friend, for these recollections of an intelligent old lady who knew the place in childhood, and gives sketches of what she remembers of it. I place this well among the medicinal wells on the authority of Lysons, who ascribes to it many miraculous sanitary qualities, although it was resorted to for its divinatory gifts chiefly.

My friend writes that this well existed in an entire state till about 1820. Over it was a little Gothic edifice, which gave the name of Porth Chapel to the spot, and Chapel Coombe to the valley and adjoining cove. It was on the western side of St. Agnes beacon, in a narrow dell descending to the sea. The situation, as is not infrequent with these buildings, is wild and weird in the extreme. Not a cottage nor a tree is to be found; a bleak heathy common, relieved by a few furze bushes, and rugged volcanic rocks, are the only objects that meet the eye.

The destruction of the chapel and its well was effected by time, and lack of faith and reverence. It is said that the principal depredators, who carried away the stone to build a hedge, said, when remonstrated with, 'What's the good of a well without water?'

The well had indeed been drained by the delvings of the miners in a work below. The name of 'Giant's Well' was given to it by the country folk, in memory of a giant who once lived near it, and was accustomed to drink of the fountain. There were the marks of his thumbs indented on a stone in the well, and near it, on another, the print of his foot, very large, and very like a footmark. Pins were dropped in with wishes as in many other parts of Cornwall."—T. Q. C.

St. Agnes, the real patroness of the well, was a most beautiful and gifted Roman lady, a descendant of a noble family. Being most ardently attached to the Christian cause she refused the hand of the son of Sempronius, then Governor of Rome, because he was not a Christian. In spite of all bribes or punishments she persistently rejected his addresses, whereupon Sempronius condemned her to be burnt. As soon as the fire was kindled, the flames divided and encircled her on every side without doing the least injury to her person. When this was seen, she was dragged from the stake, and by order of Auspitius was beheaded by the common executioner. This martyrdom took place A.D. 304, in the latter end of the reign of Diocletian, when the saint was only about thirteen years of age.

ALSIA WELL.

"This well, once of great repute, is situated in a deep bottom in the parish of St. Buryan. William Bottrell, 'an old Celt,' who has diligently and lovingly recorded the folk-lore of West Cornwall, thus speaks of it :—

'We know not if "this fount" is still regarded as a holy well; but many years ago we have often heard an aged lady, who was born and bred near Alsia, and was well acquainted with legendary lore and old customs of the district, say that in her younger days the Saint's Well of Alsia was almost as much frequented on the three first Wednesdays in May as the noted well of Chapel Uny. Mothers came from far and near with their weak and rickety children that they might be strengthened by being bathed in its waters. Moreover, the same old lady to whom we are beholdened for many of the incidents of the legend, Nancy Trenoweth (the fair daughter of the miller of Alsia), informed us that it was not unusual for these pilgrimages to be the occasion of a fight between the women of Alsia and the pilgrim mothers, when the good housewives caught the strangers dipping their precious babes into the enclosed part of the well, or the place from which the neighbours drew their drinking water.'[1] A cross formerly stood near this fountain, and its socketed pedestal was until lately to be seen.

The Alsia Well was also one of the wishing or divining sort. Of a summer's evening scores of maidens might be seen around it, eager for their turn to see what sweethearts would be united or parted, which they discovered by the fall of pebbles or pins. As the articles sank near or apart so their future was foretold; and the number of the bubbles raised bespoke the number of years before the happy or unhappy issue could befall. Another method of consulting the spirit of the well was by floating bramble leaves on it."—T. Q. C.

[1] *Traditions and Hearthside Stories of West Cornwall.* Penzance, 1870: printed by W. Cornish.

ST. AMBROSE WELL, CRANTOCK.

In the *Parochial History of Cornwall* is the following:—

"A chapel, dedicated to St. Ambrusca, formerly stood in the churchyard; and an ancient covered well, dedicated to the same saint, still exists in the centre of the church village. The building is about five feet six inches high, and about four feet wide. The opening is narrow, and protected by an iron crossbar."

This well has now been quite destroyed, and "St. Ambrose Villa" covers the spot where the little building once stood. The stream, however, still flows.

ST. ANNE'S WELL, WHITESTONE.

This well is prettily situated in a hollow in the churchyard at the south-east of the church, surrounded and overshadowed by beautiful trees; the building is at present in very good condition, having been restored in comparatively late years (about 1883). The interior is composed of loosely built stones, only the arched roof being mortared; at the back is an ancient niche, and over this a curiously carved stone. The roof of the well is entirely overgrown with grass and wild flowers; the arched doorway, about four feet high, has the words "Saint Anna" carved round it, and over the doorway is another niche: the name of the well was carved at its restoration, but several bits of the building were brought from other parts; the stone cross which stands on the point of the roof is said to have belonged to some neighbouring church. The water has never been known to fail, and is still used for baptisms.

ST. AUSTEN'S WELL, LESNEWTH.

This well lies in the valley between Lesnewth and Davidstow, and, as is the case with so many of these holy wells, not far from the spot on which an ancient chapel once stood; "Hendra Chapel" being still the name of the farmhouse near. Maclean says: "It is a fine spring of water, and forms the source of the brook which on that side forms the parish boundary". The well is now enclosed with "pitching-stones"; but the sexton of the parish says that in his younger days he had been informed that a wall surrounded it; when he was appointed sexton (some fifty years since) he always fetched from St. Austen's Well all water required for use at baptisms, as his predecessors had done before him; but of late years this custom has been discontinued.

HOLY WELL ON ST. BELLARMIN'S TOR.

Many Cornish historians mention the fact that on the summit of St. Bellarmin's Tor, in the parish of Cardynham, were the remains of a chapel and well. Now there are no more distinct traces of masonry than a few stones lying round about : the spring still exists, but no building covers it. Some little while ago two gentlemen visited the Tor, and after scraping and digging among the stones for many hours succeeded in bringing to light some lime which had the appearance of having been used in mortar; this showed traces that the hand of man had been at work on that desolate spot, but there is now nothing to mark its former sacredness.

ST. BERNARD'S WELL, ST. STEPHEN'S IN BRANNEL.

St. Bernard's Well, an ancient well or baptistery, the waters of which were said to possess medicinal qualities, was destroyed by mining.

HOLY WELL, BLISLAND.

In the *Parochial History of Cornwall* is the following notice of this well :—"At Teason, about three furlongs to the east of the church, are the remains of a chapel or oratory, and a large well with a stone roof. Of the chapel, which was fourteen feet long by nine in breadth, the foundations remain, also one of the chamfered door jambs, the arch-stone is impost, and the stoup. The well is in good preservation; the spring rises at the inner corner, and flowing through the doorway forms a pool on the outside; it is locally known as Holy Well."

This well is probably in much the same condition at present as it was at the time of the above description; its late rector, writing of it in the summer of 1891, says:—"It is at an old ruinated chapel, in a lonely spot on Tregenna estate. Its water flows from beneath the building under a circular piece of granite in the end wall. The well is walled round with granite. The water has been thought good for weak eyes, and has been used for that purpose."

According to Maclean, "there has always been some superstition connected with this field" [the field called Chapel Park, on which the chapel and well stand]. "From generation to generation it has been believed that it should never be broken for tillage, and that whenever this was done some frightful disaster would befall the family of the person by whom the act was committed. This year (1878) there was grown in it a crop of corn; and in the time of harvest the son of the farmer, a boy of about ten years of age, whilst climbing up to take down a scythe, fell, together with the scythe, and falling on it cut his knee so severely that it was found necessary to amputate the leg above it, thus strengthening the superstition."[1]

1 Maclean.

HOLY WELL, BODMIN.

"A mile or so above Scarlet's Well, in the Fairwash coombe, is this clear and perennial fountain, still giving its name to the field in which it is situated. The well is not now, if it ever was, enclosed by any masonry; but the limpid stream runs into a granite trough, the overflow irrigating the grass below. It had great repute among the dead and gone folk of Bodmin; still the aged retain some remembrance of it, and tell me how in youth they used to frequent Holy Well to divine their future by rushes from the marsh below, tied crosswise and (with a now forgotten verse) put to float upon its water. On a recent visit I searched for votive coin or pin, but found none. Hydromancy is dead in this generation." —T. Q. C.

BRASS WELL, MEVAGISSEY.

This well deserves mention on account of its former reputation. It was at one time spoken of as the "Tunbridge Wells of the West"; its waters, which were strong chalybeate, resembling the Tunbridge springs. The name "Brass Well" arose from the peculiar appearance of the sulphureous scum which floated on its surface. Many were the cures resulting from the use of Brass Well waters according to old accounts, but none have happened within living memory. The well still exists (on Trelevan or Trelevean), and is known still by its old name; but its ancient fame is forgotten, and it is never now used medicinally.

HOLY WELL, CHAPEL FARM, ST. BREWARD.

"This dilapidated building stands in a sequestered valley, near a tenement still keeping the name of Chapel, in the parish of St. Breward. This suggests that the spot was once the site of some religious edifice; in confirmation of which the occupier relates that in building his present abode from the remains of a former house on the same spot, many stones were used which had the appearance of having formed part of the arched doors and windows of an ecclesiastical building.

The old well, supplied by a perennial spring, is still visited on certain stated occasions by those afflicted with inflamed eyes, and other infirmities, having faith in its powers. The favour of the presiding saint is first bespoken by the offering of a farthing or pin. This faith has much declined. I visited the well on 8th August, 1856, and a careful groping in the muddy bottom only rewarded me by a few pins; though in former times these and other votive offerings may have furnished no inconsiderable revenue to the adjacent chapelry. On this visit I made a sketch of the well, which was engraved by my friend, J. T. Blight.[1] Now,

[1] *Ancient Crosses, etc., of Cornwall*, p. 88.

in August, 1881, I find that the delvings of the miners and granite masons have drained the spring, and the old structure is tottering to its fall. My original drawing, here preserved, is not without small value, as preserving a memory of an interesting relic.

According to Oliver's *Monasticon*, there were two chapels in this parish in A.D. 1442, dedicated to St. Michael and St. James, and probably there was one of them adjacent to the well."---T. Q. C.

This seems all the more likely from the fact of the arched stones, etc., being dug up at a very short distance from the well. The most reasonable theory is that the holy well was dedicated either to St. Michael or St. James, and not to St. Breward; for the latter saint never dwelt in this part, and his name being given to the parish is due to the fact that a church was given to the priory of Tywardreath by William Peverell, then lord of the manor, and dedicated to St. Breward de Hamthethi.[1] No reliable records can be found of him, and his history is almost entirely unknown.

In 1891, on visiting this well, we found it in better preservation than we had expected, considering that ten years ago it was "tottering to its fall". At the back was a large opening made by miners, who, though they have not quite drained the spring, which is of most beautiful quality, have materially lessened its volume; but, in spite

[1] Maclean's *History of Trigg Minor.*

Holy Well, Chapel Farm, St. Breward.

of this, it never ceases to flow, and, conducted by "shutes" to the back of the farm, supplies the house throughout the year.

There is a large thorn growing over the well, the root being inside, and the trunk coming through the walls. The interior is lined with beautiful ferns, and the front surrounded by ferns and nettles. The height of the arched entrance is three feet seven and a half inches.

The old customs have fallen into disuse; no pins or farthings are ever thrown in the water now, nor could we hear of any superstition left connected with the spot; but information is scarce and difficult to get from the country people. One fact we noted particularly, that when inquiring our way to St. Breward's Holy Well, the people did not know it by that name, but spoke of it as "the Holy Well at Chapel". The latter place is nearly a mile from St. Breward Church Town.

Not more than two miles from Chapel is Michaelstow, with its holy well. One of the two chapels spoken of by Oliver may have been here, for two miles in a Cornish parish is comparatively nothing. In which case the well on Chapel farm must have been St. James'. But this is merely supposition.

THE WELL OF ST. CARANTOCUS.

This saint was a son of a Welsh king named Careticus. In about 432, Carantocus joined St. Patrick in Ireland, to help him in converting the Irish; he stayed there many years, but returned to Cornwall in 460, with a large number of Irish hermits. "Karantoc constructed an oratory for himself, in the place which was called Guerith Karantauc," says Leland. "This land must have been assigned to the dignified hermit by the owner of the soil under the permission of the king. Both, therefore, must have been as much Christians in profession as Carantoc was one in zeal," adds Whitaker.

St. Carantoc, like St. Piran, settled by the North Sea, but a little more to the east. He gave his name to the parish, fixed his cell by the church, was buried in it, according to Whitaker, and soon after his death the College of Crantock sprung up in his honour and to his memory.

"This College of Crantock may pretend to as much antiquity as any college in Oxford, since it appears to have had great revenues at the time of the inquisition before mentioned, 1294; though it hath been so unfortunate not to have been so long lived, by reason of the great quantities of sea-sand blown up from the Gannell creek by the wind, as Hollingshed saith." Nothing is now left of the college, or the cell; but the holy well still exists, in the centre of the village, near the church, covered with a curious bee-hive shaped structure with a door. The villagers use the water for all household purposes, and when a pump was erected still preferred the sacred water. It has never been said to have possessed any special virtues.

CARDYNHAM HOLY WELL.

This well "is north of the church village, and at the distance of a quarter of a mile. Ruinous beyond repair, it still keeps marks of having been one of our largest and most important holy wells. Several years ago I visited and explored it with my friend Blight, and can add nothing to his description and picture. I found it still further decayed on a later visit to it. A plot of ground eighty feet long and forty-two feet broad is walled up to the height of the top of the well, on which, according to tradition, there was a church or chapel."—T.Q.C.

Polwhele says: "The Holy Well at Cardynham was sacred before the saints"; and Drew in his *History of Cornwall* speaks of the chapel in the following paragraph: "It is reported that there were formerly two churches in this parish besides that now extant, which is comparatively a modern building. One of these was on the site of old Cardinham Castle, the other at a holy well which was venerated before the saints probably made their appearance in Cornwall. Of the former no memorials whatever remain, and of the latter we know little but from the reports of tradition. At present this venerable well is walled in and arched over with moorstone, exhibiting some ruins, which, according to tradition, belonged to an ancient chapel. Admitting these places of public worship to have existed, they must be reckoned among the most ancient devoted to Christianity in Cornwall."

Thirty-five years ago a corner of this chapel was still standing, so say the villagers; twenty years ago the spot bore the appearance of a burying-ground (probably owing to the fallen stones, all grown over by moss and grass); and about seventeen years ago a plantation of trees was made upon the very site where the chapel once stood. The stones of that lingering corner were taken down and used in the building of outhouses on the farm of Trenance; for the farmer of that time, wishing to do the work as quickly and inexpensively as possible, of course gladly took the shaped stones so ready to hand; however, shame, or some other cause, seems to have guided him in the arrangement of his sacrilegious booty, for he caused the carved faces of the stones to be built in against other stones, thus concealing their value and their original service. At an adjacent farm are also some stones which had been brought from the chapel—a piece of arched granite which had probably formed a window, also another piece of heavy granite which had evidently been a stoup for holy water, cut from a large block of shapeless stone which had the appearance of having been built into a wall. An old doorway was also here, soon to be pulled down and rebuilt, having an arch of shaped granite likely to have been brought from the chapel. Until about forty years ago water was still brought from the holy well for baptisms; now its use is not altogether so sacred, being often utilised as a butter and cream cooler. The description given above is still a very good one; no apparent change has taken place, except, perhaps, that a wooden door now secures the opening, and is furnished with a lock and key; the latter being kept in all probability by the owner of the butter and cream.

WELL AT CASTLE HORNECK.

This is a curious little well at the side of the road, with two odd pillars, one on either side of it,—one, only a shaped block of granite, the other a carved stone, but palpably not originally intended to stand in the position it now occupies. The top of the well, which is level with the road, has been until quite recently open; now a roughly hewn block of granite covers it, but, judging from the appearance of the pillars, one would imagine that in bygone times it had been regularly roofed in, particularly as there are two granite steps to get down to the entrance of the well from the road. The well faces the hedge. The water was considered very good for sore eyes.

HOLY WELL AT CHAPEL HALTON.

Two chapels once existed at Halton, one dedicated to St. Ildract or Indractus, and one to St. Dominica, the sister of the latter saint, and patron saint of the parish of St. Dominick; the parish church being dedicated to her by Bishop Brownescombe in 1259. These two saints lived as hermits in Somersetshire, and died violent deaths.

No trace of either of the chapels now remains; only a little holy well, which probably was connected with one or the other, situated by the side of the road leading from Chapel Farm to the river Tamar, which is a few hundred yards below.

The well, which has granite arches, has also a niche at the back for the figure of the patron saint. A trough which stands near the door has no original connection with it, but was placed there recently for the benefit of cattle. The structure is now in a neglected and overgrown condition.

CHAPEL UNY WELL.

"This famous well is in the parish of Sancreed, not far from the Land's End. The water wells forth, but the building which once covered it is demolished. Dr. Borlase says[1] that 'as a witness of its having done remarkable cures, it has a chapel adjoining to it, dedicated to St. Eunius; the ruins of which, consisting of much carved stone, bespeak it to have been formerly of no little note. The water has the reputation of drying humours as well as healing wounds.'

He adds that, 'the common people (of this as well as other countries) will not be content to attribute the benefit they receive to ordinary means; there must be something marvellous in all their cures. I happened, luckily, to be at this well upon the last day of the year, on which, according to vulgar opinion, it exerts its principal and most salutary powers. Two women were here who came from a neighbouring parish, and were busily employed in bathing a child. They both assured me that people who had a mind to receive any benefit from St. Euny's well, must come and wash upon the first three Wednesdays

[1] Borlase, *Nat. Hist. of Cornwall*, p. 31. (Date A.D. 1757.)

in May. But to leave folly to its own delusion, it is certainly very gracious in Providence to distribute a remedy for so many disorders in a quality so universally found as cold is in every unmixed well water.'

Dr. Paris describes it as it was some sixty years ago. The ruins of a chapel or baptistery were observable near, and the water of the well was then supposed to possess many miraculous virtues, especially in infantile mesenteric disease. They were dipped on the three first Wednesdays in May, and drawn through the pool three times *against the sun* and three times on the surrounding grass in the same direction.[1]

This well, according to this distinguished physician and chemist, like Madron, does not contain any mineral impregnation, but must derive its force and virtue from the tonic effects of cold, and from the firm faith of the devotees. The credulous still go here to divine the future in the appearance of the bubbles which a pin or pebble sends up.

'Two or three carved stones are all that remain of the old structure; and at the stated times when the well is sought for divination and cure, a bath is formed by impounding the water by turves cut from the surrounding moor. The country people know it as the Giant's Well.'"[2]—T. Q. C.

1 *Guide to Mount's Bay*, etc., p. 82.

2 Halliwell's *Rambles in Western Cornwall*, p. 191.

Now it is simply an open spring, all remains of the building are gone, and the site obliterated. The water is not used for any special purpose, and the well is only remembered for its past importance.

CHAPEL WELL, TOWAN.

"This well is on Towan farm, a little to the south of St. Austell town. I went on a visit to it in the year 1882. Winding to the left, close by a small wayside inn with a curious signboard, 'The London Apprentice,'—a name suggestive of some tale of wild roystering and lawless riot, or of venture and success—then, turning up a hill, long and steep, the deeply-cut hedges, full of cryptogamic greenery, I arrived at the farmhouse, where I luckily found an intelligent boy, who knew all about the well, and where it was. After clearing a few hedges I found it in what is now a morass, plashy and full of rush and marsh plants. The well was buried in a bush growth of ivy and bramble; the latter had never known the pruning-hook for generations, and had grown with such unconstrained licence that the long branches with their formidable prickles were more than I could encounter, unarmed as I was. I had prepared myself with sketch-book and drawing materials, but they were useless. By carefully turning back as much of this lavish drapery as I could, I made out a stately well, built of shaped and shapely granite slabs. The doorway was finished upwards by a chamfered, I should say, equilateral arch. The water flooded the whole of the floor of the enclosed space; the roof was arched like the doorway, and in the end wall was a neat and large bracket pedestal, evidently for the effigy of a saint. As well as I could make out in the darkness, this corbel-like projection was fluted, or otherwise ornamented; the front was, I judged, highly peaked, like St. Cyr's of Luxulyan.

The boy had never heard of elf or saint in connection with it, and could tell me no story of its ever being frequented for health, or fortune-telling. Its position and surroundings spoke of long neglect and desolation. The massive nature of its construction has wonderfully preserved this once beautiful fountain from destruction, and very little cost and care would restore it. I made its condition known to its owner, Sir C. Graves-Sawle, Bart., of Penrice."—T. Q. C.

Since the foregoing account was written, the covering of brambles and nettles has been carefully cleared away: and the well stands, one of the largest and handsomest we found in the county, in a most wonderful state of preservation. The description given of it is a very exact one. The carved bracket in the interior is perfect. On the left-hand side of the doorway is a square hole, perhaps made to hold a cup or drinking-vessel; but, of course, one can only conjecture.

As in many instances when the well is called *Chapel* Well, this one is situated in a large roughly enclosed space, where a chapel also may formerly have stood; and knowing this to have often been the case, we searched carefully, and examined the few large stones lying about, for traces of such a building, but could find none.

CHAPEL WELL, ST. WENN.

On Carenza Wartha estate there was in former days a consecrated well, dedicated to St. Mary Magdalene, and a free chapel stood near. There are now no traces whatever of either building; the spring indeed still remains, and is deliciously clear and cold; but the chapel is considered to have been destroyed in the time of the civil wars.

An old woman of the village, speaking of the well, said that its water is thought very highly of in cases of illness, and she has known it to be carried scores of miles for the benefit of invalids at a distance. The spring never runs dry, and during one drought, when the ordinary village well was entirely dried up, the villagers came to Chapel Well for all water for domestic purposes, as did also the farmers for water for their cattle, and all found sufficiency.

Another villager, on being interrogated, said that he understood there had once been a burying-ground near, which had been much dug since those days, and bones had been found; he also said that shaped stones had been discovered lying about the well, which fact favours the idea that there was originally a building over the spring. These stones were collected by Mr. Rashleigh, a late vicar, and preserved in his own grounds.

ST. CLARE'S WELL

Is in Kenwyn parish. Hals gives this account of it :—

"Near Edles or Ideless, *i.e.*, narrow breadth, formerly the voke lands of a considerable manor, taxed in Domesday book as aforesaid, privileged then with the jurisdiction of a court leet, is yet to be seen the ruins and downfalls of St. Clare's consecrated and walled well, chapelwise built by the nuns of the nunnery house of poor Clares in Truro, called An-hell, *i.e.*, the Hall ; but yet, alas ! as tradition saith, they were not so poor as their rule obligeth them to be, for in the walls of this well they had deposited or hid away considerable sums of money, which, by tradition or some dream, was discovered, *tempore* James II, to some of the inhabitants of this parish, who one night pulled down the walls and totally defaced this chapel well in quest thereof, and probably succeeded in their design and undertaking, for soon after some poor labourers in agriculture became rich farmers and landed men and others."

The saint from whom this well took its name was, according to Hals, "a lady of honourable lineage," dwelling in the city of Assisum, Italy (see St. Clare's Well, near Liskeard), who gave herself up to a religious course of life, and established colleges in various spots, called *the Order of the Poor Clares.*

The well, which must have been an unusually elaborate structure of its sort, as we are told it was a "walled well, chapelwise built," has no trace of stonework now remaining; in fact, for some time we could gain no tidings of any such well in the village of Edless; but after interrogating several persons on the subject, we elicited the fact that there was a field called St. Clare's Close, in which was a never-failing spring of good water; on visiting the field we saw this same spring bubbling up from the ground; no building, no stones, nor slightest trace of any former importance was to be seen, and the surrounding earth was trodden down by bullocks; but the quality of the water was greatly praised; and this spot is in all probability the site of St. Clare's Chapel Well.

ST. CLEER WELL.

"When I visited this interesting well in 1850, and made the sketches of it here appended, it was a very pretty group of ruins. The cross, of Latin form, about seven feet high and *recercelé* on both

sides, stood near the well, the front of which, partly enveloped in ivy, was fairly entire.[1] The arches and buttresses, well moulded, showed it to

[1] See Gilbert's *Hist. of Corn.*, vol. ii, p. 947

have been once a work of great skill, labour and cost. The entrance was by a double arch, the central mullion being imperfect. The back of the well was down, and the space partly filled with the sharply-cut and well-fashioned ruins. The water is good and plentiful. I tried to gather something

of the legends connected with the well, but was only told tantalisingly that there were many strange stories about it, that it was still held to have miraculous virtues, and was resorted to by the halt and the blind. I could get no confirmation of the statement that it was once a bowsening pool.

St. Cleer Well, 1891.

Many of our Cornish wells have, as in the case of St. Nun's in Pelynt,[1] some tradition connected with them, intended by those who first gave them currency to stay the hand of the destroyer. This has been so saved that it would not be difficult to effect an entire restoration from the ruins which lie scattered round. I learnt from a native of the parish that some of the stones of the well have been at various times carted away to serve meaner purposes; but they have, by some mysterious agency, been brought back again during the night. This account describes St. Cleer Well as it was in the year 1850.

In 1864 it was restored by the family of Rogers of Penrose, near Helstone, to the memory of the Rev. John Jope, for sixty-seven years vicar of the parish, as is recorded on a slab in the wall."—T. Q. C.

The saint from whom the parish, and also the well, is named, is St. Clare, or St. Clear, who was, according to Hals, " born of honourable lineage at the city of Assisum in Italy, in the province of Umbra; and being from her youth a practiser of the Christian religion with great zeal, she became desirous to follow a religious course of life; and to that end applied herself to St. Francis, who lived in that city, and made known the same to him; who greatly commended her for it, and soon after consecrated her a nun by cutting off her hair, and

[1] See p. 175.

apparelling her in the habit of the order of the Nuns of St. Benedict. He carried her to the monastery of St. Paul in that city, which was of that order, where she remained till St. Francis had repaired the church of St. Damian, without the city, in a solitary place, wherein he set her; in which she was closed up in the love of Jesus Christ, and there begun or set up a college of virgins called *the Order of the Poor Clares of St. Benedict*, under the solemn vows of obedience, poverty, and chastity, according to the rule of St. Francis."

St. Cleer's Well is said to have belonged to a nunnery, once extant either in this parish or at Liskeard, of one of the three Orders of Poor Clares. The building is in a very complete state; but, unfortunately for its character as a well, a large block of granite now covers the water. The back of the well appears to be mostly, if not entirely, the old building. It stands on a walled-in plot of ground by the roadside; and certainly, from its form, may have once been used as a bowsening pool.

ST. CLETHER'S WELL.

"Not far from the church of St. Clether, in a field called Chapel Park, are the ruins of an ancient chapel, the altar-table of which was not long since complete, but is now thrown down. Little or nothing is known of its history. It had, according to Blight, some interesting features. It was built with a kind of slate stone with granite dressings. Its length was eighteen feet, and its breadth sixteen feet; the jambs of the door had deep plain mouldings.

Opposite the door stands the altar, composed of a slab of granite as the *mensa*, four feet two inches long, two feet two inches broad, and four feet and a half inch thick. A plain moulding is carved round the edge. It is supported by the wall and four hewn granite blocks."—T. Q. C.

This chapel, which is the largest in Cornwall, was the cell and oratory of St. Cleder or Clederus, a son of Brechan, and the original parish church; in former times the spot was evidently enclosed, and the ground raised.

The well attached to the chapel is in very perfect condition, and has a domed roof. No tradition or legend hangs about it; but the water, which is always, when possible, used for baptisms, has never been known to fail.

Through neglect this interesting and beautiful well, in its wild and picturesque situation, is falling into ruin ; the water, not having a proper channel to run in, overflows all the ground around, and makes the spot almost unapproachable. One wonders how the possessor of such an interesting antiquity can be so indifferent.

ST. COHAN'S WELL, MERTHER.

St. Cohan, the guardian saint of Merther church, "was murdered and slayne for the Christian religion as a martyr," according to Hals, who describes him as "one St. Cohan, a Britaine of this parish, whose *little well* and consecrated chapell annexed thereto was lately extant upon the lands of *Egles Merther* barton, though now in a manner demolished by greedy searchers for money"; he goes on to say, "I take this martyr to have been slayne by the Saxons, upon forethought malice".

Whitaker, in his *Cathedral of Cornwall*, writes: "This unknown saint appears from his *well* to have lived as a hermit at the place, and from the *tradition* to have been slain at his hermitage,—not, indeed, by the *pagan* Saxons in some very early invasion of Cornwall, as no such invasion appears either certainly or probably to have been made; but in some personal pique by that private Saxon assuredly who at Athelstan's conquest of Cornwall settled in the house so singularly denominated Tre-Sawsen, or the Saxon's house, and lying about a mile to the south of the well. From his murder and character as a hermit and a saint, he was honoured for a martyr by the neighbouring Christians, just as we have seen Edward, Sidwell,

Melor, and Melian, honoured before. His hermitage afterwards, as we have seen, equally practised at St. Mawes, became a 'consecrated chapell,' and was therefore 'annexed' to the well. The well was thus formed like one equally noticed by Hals in the parish of Kenwyn."

St. Cohan's Well is still to be seen, but no building remains over it, nor is there any sign of the ruins of a hermitage; it is situated in a pretty little secluded nook in the corner of a field to the south of the church, and is separated from the rest of the field by a high hedge; the enclosure thus made being probably the space occupied by the former hermitage of St. Cohan when it stood near the well. The water is still fetched from thence for baptisms.

WELL OF COLURIAN.

This well, in the parish of Ludgvan, was purely curative, and very little now seems to be remembered of its past notability, though it must have been at one time held in great repute, if one may judge from references made to it as a well of recognised virtues in histories of Cornwall. Drew says of it: "This spring is strongly impregnated, and is justly remarkable for benefits which have resulted from its use. The bed through which this water flows is a loose pebbly ground, mixed with a gravelly clay full of ochrous iron mineral, which gives it a peculiar taste and smell." Upon this water Dr. Borlase tried experiments, which he has detailed in his *Natural History of Cornwall*, as follows: "In the morning before the water is stirred there is a skin or film on the surface, of a rainbow colour, shooting to and fro, by which it may be presumed that there is sulphur or naphtha mixed with this water, which rises and settles on the top. In a calm but not very warm morning on 7th August, 1734, before six o'clock, I found the water, both in the enclosed well and without where it ran exposed to the air, almost blood warm, and the common water, which runs nine feet from the chalybeate, as cold as snow,

. . . by which it is to be concluded that the chalybeate spring derives a sensible heat from the bed of iron, vitriol, and pyrites, which it passes through. Two persons, of which I have sufficient proof, by drinking and washing the part affected, have been cured of king's evil."

On inquiry we ascertained that Colurian stream is still in existence, but we could not hear that it is still resorted to for cures.

ST. CONSTANTINE'S HOLY WELL.

The legend of this well is given by Hunt in his *Popular Romances of the West of England*, as follows: "In the parish of St. Merran, or Meryn, near Padstow, are the remains of the church of St. Constantine, and the holy well of that saint. It had been an unusually hot and dry summer, and all the crops were perishing through want of water. The people inhabiting the parish had grown irreligious, and many of them sadly profane. The drought was a curse upon them for their wickedness. Their church was falling into ruin, their well was foul, and the arches over it were decayed and broken. In their distress, the wicked people, who had reviled the word of God, went to their priest for aid.

"'There is no help for thee unless thou cleanest the holy well.'

"They laughed him to scorn. The drought continued, and they suffered want. To the priest they went again.

"'Cleanse the well,' was his command, 'and see the power of the blessing of the first Christian emperor.'

"That cleansing a dirty well should bring them rain, they did not believe. The drought continued, the rivers were dry; the people suffered thirst.

"'Cleanse the well, wash, and drink,' said the priest, when they again went to him.

"Hunger and thirst made the people obedient. They went to the task. Mosses and weeds were removed, and the filth cleansed. To the surprise of all, beautifully clear water welled forth. They drank the water and prayed, and then washed themselves and were refreshed. As they bathed their bodies, parched with heat, in the cool stream which flowed from the well, the heavens clouded over, and presently rain fell, turning all hearts to the true faith."

Whitaker, writing of the saint, who was also a king, says: "How Constantine the king became a martyr we know not. He certainly could not become one in the just sense of the word. He was killed, therefore, by some one in his retirement, out of resentment for the past. But where was his retirement? Not, as we naturally suppose at first, in the parish denominated from him. At the church of this parish was no 'religious house,' as Dr. Borlase, misled by Tanner, supposes there was. The very words of Doomsday Book, cited by him to prove there was, prove there was none. 'Sanctus Constantinus,' is language appropriated to a church merely parochial, while the collegiate or conventual church is distinguished by the addition of 'Clerici,' or 'Canonici' of the saint, 'habet dimidium hidæ terræ, etc.' And the *Valor* of Pope Nicholas concurs, noticing 'ecclesia Sancti Constantini,' just as it notices all merely parochial churches. But at another point of Cornwall was it that Constantine lived as a hermit, even at St. Merin, near Padstow. There, and there only, 'is yet extant St. Constantine's Well, strong built of stone, and arched over,' and near it are 'the ruines of an old church, chapell, and cemitery, pertayninge thereto, dedicated to St. Constantine'; a chapel (I presume) to Padstow, as St. Merin is no parish in Pope Nicholas' *Valor*, the original chapel of the district, as tradition points its finger at it for the original church of the parish; and a chapel nearly buried now in the encroaching waves of the sea."

The Rev. W. S. Lach-Szyrma avers that Constantine "died in penitence and sanctity"; he does not speak of any martyrdom, but describes him as follows: "The Cornish King Constantine—to whose memory the parish of St. Constantine, and also probably the chapelries in Illogan and St. Merryn, are dedicated—lived two centuries after the Emperor Constantine the Great. He was a Cornishman, son of Padarn, King of Cornwall, who reigned here about the time when Cerdic the Saxon was founding the kingdom of Wessex, and, we may add, that of England. Constantine was king after his father; but seems to have been involved in some political crime, probably to secure himself in the crown, and killed two children of the royal family. Misfortune followed him, and he was struck with repentance. His wife died, or, as some say, he divorced her; possibly both may have occurred.

King Constantine, grieved at his sin and weary of sovereignty, like a second St. Gerome abdicated and retired to the monastery of St. David's. From here he went to some distant land (probably Scotland), founded a monastery, and died in penitence and sanctity. His feast is observed in Cornwall on 9th or 10th March."

No trace of the well of St. Constantine could we find in July, 1891,—at least none of which one could feel certain. At about a stone's throw from the ruined chapel, on lower ground and surrounded by marsh, was a little mound, grown over by grass, and rushes, and weeds; on pushing back some of this growth there appeared to be two low walls,—whether of masonry or mud we could not tell, and a very slight covering over it near the back; but if these were really the remains of a building erected over the spring, there seemed to be no place for the water to run from it. There was a running stream; but although quite close, it appeared to have nothing to do with the little mound.

The ruins of the ancient chapel were in much the same condition probably as they have been for the last half century,—standing out, black and lonely, on the desolate sand-hills, with the sea just beyond. They appeared to be strong, and likely to stand for many years to come; the doorway was left complete as regards shape, and an alcove or recess still remained, hidden by a large elder tree.

ST. CUBY'S WELL, DULOE.

In the parish of Duloe, on the road which leads from Sandplace to Duloe Church, at one time stood the consecrated well of St. Cuby. This saint, who has been called also *Keby* by some of his biographers, was the son of Solomon, a Christian king or chieftain of Cornwall. According to the Rev. S. Baring-Gould, Solomon was a son of Geraint, and his wife was a sister of St. Non. St. Cuby at an early age gave himself up to learning and religion; he renounced all claim to his father's kingdom, to which he undoubtedly had the right, in favour of his brother's family, and settled at Tregony for a short time, after which he visited Ireland, and finally went to Anglesea, where he died. The well of St. Cuby was a spring of water on the left-hand side of the above road, which flowed into a circular basin of granite, carved and ornamented round the edge with the figures of dolphins, and on the lower part with the figure of a griffin; it is in shape somewhat like a font, with a drain for the carrying off of the water.

The well at one time was very much respected, and treated with reverence by the neighbouring people, who believed that some dire misfortune would befal the person who should attempt to remove it. Tradition says that a ruthless fellow once went with a team of oxen for the purpose of removing the basin; on reaching the spot one of the oxen fell down dead, which so alarmed the man that he desisted from the attempt.[1] In spite of this tradition, however, the basin has been moved, probably when the new road was cut, and was taken to the bottom of the woods on the Trenant estate; it is now placed in Trenant Park.

[1] The same story is told of St. Nun's Well, Pelynt.

ST. CUTHBERT'S, OR ST. CUBERT'S WELL

"Is in the parish of that name in the north of Cornwall, by the Bristol Channel. Hals says of it: 'A famous and well-known spring of water called Holy Well (so named, the inhabitants say, for that the virtues of this water were discovered on All Hallows' Day). The same stands in a dark cavern of the sea-cliff rocks; beneath full sea-mark on spring-tides drop down or distil continually drops of water from the white, blue, red, and green veins of those rocks; and accordingly, in the place where those drops of water fall, they swell to a lump of considerable bigness; and there petrifying to the hardness of ice, glass, or freestone, of the several colours aforesaid, according to the nature of those veins in the rock from whence they proceed.' These stalactites are hard and brittle as glass.

It must have been a well of very wide repute, as Hals tells us that people frequented it in 'incredible' numbers in summer, 'from countries far distant'.

Mr. J. C. Oliver, in his excellent *Guide to Newquay*, gives us this reliable account of the well in its present condition:—

'About two miles to the south-east of Crantock

is Holy Well, a long unbroken beach, bounded on either extremity by fine cliffs, but having a coast-line of wild and desert sandhills, the loose surface of which is continually shifting and drifting. The only signs of vegetation upon this desolate sea-shore are a few thinly-scattered sea-rushes, either struggling to retain their hold or half buried by the drift.

'This sandy dune runs inland a considerable distance towards Cubert, and thence across to Perran. During a strong breeze off-shore the drift of loose sand is perfectly blinding. But that which gives to Holy Well its chief interest, at least in a legendary point of view, is the holy well itself, which will be found situated in one of the caverns of the eastern cliffs. It is a somewhat curious place. After passing over a few boulders the mouth of the cave will be reached, where steps will be found leading up to the well.

'This rock-formed cistern is of a duplicate form, consisting of two wells, having a communication existing between them. The supply of water is from above; and this water, being of a calcareous nature, has coated the rock with its earthy deposits, giving to the surrounding walls and to the well itself a variegated appearance of white, green and purple. Above and beyond the well will be seen a deep hole extending into the cliff.

'The legend respecting the well is, that in olden times mothers on Ascension Day brought their deformed or sickly children here, and dipped them in, at the same time passing them through the aperture connecting the two cisterns; and thus, it is said, they became healed of their disease or deformity. It would seem that other classes also believed virtue to reside in its water; for it is said that the cripples were accustomed to leave their crutches in the hole at the head of the well.'

This well has Nature only for its architect, no mark of man's hand being seen in its construction; a pink enamelled basin, filled by drippings from the stalactitic roof, forms a picture of which it is difficult to describe the loveliness. What wonder, then, that the simple folk around should endow it with mystic virtues?"—T. Q. C.

The well is supposed to have received its virtue from being accidentally touched by the reliques of the saint from whom it receives its name. It happened in this manner:—

"In 995, Alchun, Bishop of Holy Island, to secure himself from the Danish invasion, took up the corpse of St. Cuthbert"—who was born in Cumberland of British parents, about the year 600, and was raised to the dignity of abbot in the Abbey of Landisfarne—"then buried in Chester-upon-the-Street, and removed to Durham, where he fixed his see. Now, our legend saith that before this the monks of Landisfarne, being disquieted in the Danish wars, and forced by that people to wander up and down with the reliques of St. Cuthbert, resolved at last to transport themselves with them into Ireland; and on their way hither were driven into Porth Island here, and thought to have settled in this by-place. But being admonished by an oracle to return, and fix the corpse at Durham, *they* built *this church* in remembrance of their being here; and the reliques communicated their healing quality to the *holy well*, which place they accidentally touched."[1]

St. Cuthbert's church stands about a mile and a half from the well.

1 Collier's *Ecclesiastical History*, vol. i, p. 202, and Camden in *Durham R.*, 776.

ST. CYR'S WELL.

"This once fine well is a little below the parish church of Luxulyan, struggling against undeserved neglect, and, I fear, unavoidable destruction; its stones decayed and disrupted, and its basin utterly and for ever drained by the excavations necessary to form the mineral railway which passes near.

When I first knew it, many years since, its condition was fairly perfect, although a newly built house above, and a rough garden wall below, which encroached on it, had done much to spoil its picturesque surroundings. The accompanying sketch represents my early recollections of it, divested of its present ugly environment. It was then a stately little well, with a constant supply of good water, built of large cut granite blocks throughout. Outwardly it was a slightly oblong building, with a highly pitched roof of slabs overlapping inwardly to the ridge, which was rounded by slight cavettos; in front, a narrow pointedly arched doorway with two rounds from basement to point. Within was a vaulted and pointed ceiling. In the further end was a projecting corbel or bracket, which I guess may once have supported some effigy of the saint; and on the left, an oblong recess, on which were probably placed the ovations of those seeking the help of the water, or perhaps for resting the drinking vessels.

All recollections of the particular gifts of the well have vanished, all respect for its sanctity has gone, and the utter fall of its structure will soon follow."—T. Q. C.

In September, 1891, we visited this well, and found that the building had been recently carefully restored; its appearance being almost exactly the same as in the accompanying sketch. But a tank now fills the interior; and the water, of which there seems a good supply, is drawn through a tap.

We can nowhere discover what particular virtue this water possessed, nor any traditions concerning it.

HOLY WELL, DAVIDSTOWE.

The parish of Davidstowe takes its name from the patron saint of the church—David, Bishop of Menevia, in Wales, and son of St. Nun, whose parish, Altarnun, is so close at hand. The well stands in a field very near the church, and is more uncommon than beautiful; it has been restored in comparatively recent years by Michael Williams, Esq., and is now in a very good state of preservation, although to a certain extent overgrown with rushes and weeds. (Maclean, in his *History of Cornwall*, says that Mr. Williams caused some of the stones used in its restoration to be brought from the ruins of an ancient chapel in the adjoining parish of Lesnewth.) It is a fairly large well, being low and broad, with a rounded back and sides, and a straight frontage; the former are composed of loosely built stones, the latter of granite. Some idea of its shape may be gathered from the measurement of some of the principal parts. The height of the entire front is but five feet two inches, in the centre of the arch; this height is considerably lessened at the sides of the arch, being there three feet ten inches, and the whole width of the front is about thirteen feet four inches; the height of the entrance is three feet four inches. The water is not very deep, and appears to run through the well from the field; the interior is dark and gloomy, guarded by a heavy wooden door, studded with iron nails. No particular use is made of the water; it has no peculiar virtues ascribed to it that we could gather, nor is there any legend or tradition belonging to this holy well.

DUPATH WELL, ST. DOMINICK.

(*See Frontispiece.*)

"This well may be found in the parish of St. Dominick, and about a mile from the town of Callington. It is an interesting structure, built entirely of granite blocks; the roof formed, as in many other cases, by long stones laid horizontally, and overlapping each other after the manner of weather-boarding, the weight of which is supported by an internal arch, springing from rude capitals, and supported by square piers. This arch, which is chamfered near the soffit, is evidently intended to serve as a chancel arch. There is a square-headed window of two lights in the east wall, and two openings with internal splays on the west of the arch, one on each side.[1] It is twelve and a half feet in length, and eleven and a half in breadth. A portion of the front is overrun with ivy; grass and weeds grow in clumps from the chinks of the roof. The water from the springs, unconfined by any regular channel, flows through the doorway, and falls out at the east end, inundating in its course much of the surrounding soil

[1] See *Exeter Diocesan Architectural Society*, vol. iii.

and rugged pathway. The spot has a deserted look, and breathes of solitude and gloom.[1]

It was found several years since by the Rev. H. M. Rice, Rector of South-hill and Callington (an ardent antiquary, in the line of ecclesiology especially), in a very dilapidated condition. He carefully picked out the ruins lying around; and, with the carefulness of one trying to put together a dissected puzzle, succeeded in restoring the well.

This well has suffered greatly from being made the peg on which to hang modern-antique fable. The country people know nothing of Siward and Githa,[2] who are purely the creation of individual fancy. Mr. Kempthorne, long a resident of Callington, has inquired among the eld, and can find no trace of such a story; and Mrs. Rice, the widow of the restorer of the well, says that her husband would most assuredly have embodied in his paper any reputed mystic qualities or local traditional tales had any such existed."—T. Q. C.

According to the *Parochial History of Cornwall* the tradition connected with this well was as follows:—" A duel was fought here between two Saxons, named Gotlieb and Sir Colan, as rival candidates for a young lady. Gotlieb was a private gentleman of considerable wealth; while Sir Colan, though a knight, was poor. The

[1] See Blight's *Ancient Crosses and Antiquities in East Cornwall. Ib., Remarks on Well Chapels of Cornwall.*

[2] See Hawker's *Ballads*, p. 21, 1869.

father of the lady wished her to marry Gotlieb, on account of his wealth; but she preferred Sir Colan, whom she had known from childhood. Sir Colan received the first wound, but ultimately overcame Gotlieb and killed him. The contest was long and desperate; Sir Colan's wound would have healed but for his impatience, to which he fell a victim." There are several versions of this romantic story, the names differing in some cases, and usually the victorious one is described as surviving the effects of the duel, and building Dupath Well as an act of atonement for his sin and a witness of his repentance. In addition to the chapels dedicated, one to St. Dominica and the other to St. Ildractus, in this parish, there was one dedicated to St. Ethelred; it seems very probable that it may have been on the Dupath estate and in the vicinity of this holy well; and to bear out this supposition a late tenant has asserted that he occasionally turned up carved stones while ploughing near it.

ST. ENDELLION'S WELL.

Endellient, one of the numerous children of Brechan, a king in Wales, gave name to the parish of St. Endellion, and also to the well ; but whether this latter was gifted with any particular virtue, there is no record to show ; there seems to be no remembered legend nor tradition connected with it, nor is there any building over it to mark its former importance. The spring, however, is never failing, even in the driest seasons, and is in common use by the villagers, who are dependent on it for their water supply. It is by the side of a narrow lane, unfrequented, except by the drawers of water.

ST. EUNIUS' WELL.

At the foot of Carn Brea Hill, and not far from the Church of Redruth, is a well dedicated to St. Eunius. A stone cross formerly stood near it.

Now it is a rugged little well, with no regular building. A moor-stone covers it, and round is a sort of curb of rough granite, with an iron bar running along. At the back is a newer stone, bearing the date 1842.

There used to be ascribed to the water the virtue that whoever was baptised in it would never be ignominiously hanged; but now no recollection of this exists, nor reverence for its sanctity. The water is much used, because it is considered better than "pumpen" water.

FAIRIES' WELL, BLISLAND.

This well is on a wastrel at the end of a short lane near the village of Tregenna; its name disposes one to conclude that it had its superstitious frequenters in times past, but there is probably nothing "saintly" connected with it.

FAIRY WELL, CARBIS BAY.

This is a wishing-well of some note in the district; people even now go there to drop in crooked pins, and wish. It is only a square hole in the ground high up on the cliffs, at the base of an overhanging rock, situated at the end of a nut grove; a stream runs along the side, and a little of it flows into the well by a gutter.

ST. GEORGE'S WELL, PADSTOW.

There is, at a short distance from the town of Padstow, a well called St. George's Well, which is never known to be dry. It is a mere spring which gushes from a rock. The legend is that the water gushed forth immediately St. George had trodden on the spot, and has never ceased to flow.

GIANT'S WELL ON ST. MICHAEL'S MOUNT.

There is a well on this mount which was in former days named "Giant's" Well, on account of the giant Cormelian, or Cormoran, who inhabited the spot. The well, or cistern, is excavated in the rock; it is still in existence, but is now known by the title of "Jack the Giant Killer's Well," and is fairly well lined with pins thrown there by persons desirous of procuring their wishes. The conclusion to be drawn is that the clever youth "Jack," who by stratagem ridded the mount of its monster by killing the giant Cormoran, was honoured by the change of the well's designation as a recognition of his service.

ST. GIGGY'S WELL.

Nothing now remains of this consecrated well and chapel, spoken of by Hals; nor do the inhabitants of St. Issey remember it at all. When Hals wrote, the remains were still standing; but these have totally disappeared. A copious stream of water which flows from a bank side there, is said to have been covered in long ago. This may be the sacred stream.

HOLY WELL, GOLANT.

"The wonders of Golant at the present day are a tree above the tower, a well in the porch, and a chimney in the roof. . . .

"The sacred spring which first attracted settlers to the spot is still to be seen close to the entrance of the church. It is sheltered by a rude arch of stonework, apparently of great antiquity, and is adorned with a luxuriant growth of moneywort and hart's-tongue ferns.

"The hermit's cell would appear to have occupied the site of the nave of the present church. The two arches of the chancel, which are the oldest portion of the building, would seem to show where his oratory stood. The nave must have been added when the hermit's cell was taken possession of by a colony of monks from Tywardreath, probably just after the great religious revival with which the thirteenth century began.

"The worship of wells seems to have been one of the great means of keeping up the religion of the Christians of the Eastern Church; for it was against this form of worship that the Saxons—when in power again in 960, through Athelstan—and all the Popes till 1242, passed such stringent laws.

"This would also account for our having lost all trace of the name of the British hermit who lived here, and for our having only left to us in its place the name of St. Sampson. He is said to have been a prince of British blood, who worked in Brittany, but he was not sainted until the Council of Lyons, in 1244. When the chapel of St. Sampson was built is not known, but it was confirmed to the Priory by Bishop Branscombe in 1281."[1]

When we visited the well in July, 1891, we found it in very good condition. The building, which is close to the south porch of Golant Church, is plain, with an arched doorway; this doorway faces the east, but is so very near the wall of the porch that its side and not its front is seen as one approaches. There was no water in it, but there was a distinct water-mark on the stones, and the ground at the bottom of the well was damp; a rough stone protruded at the back of the interior, but whether or not it was intended for a figure of a saint is open to conjecture.

[1] *Notes on the Parish of Golant*, by E. W. Rashleigh.

GULVAL WELL.

"'In Fosses Moor, part of the manor of Lanesely,' Hals tells us, 'is that well-known fountain called Gulfall or Wulf-all Well, *i.e.*, *help*, cure, support, or succour *all Well*, or Fountain; to which place great numbers of people, time out of mind, have resorted for pleasure and profit of their health, as the credulous country people do in these days, not only to drink the waters thereof, but to inquire after the life or death of their absent friends: where, being arrived, they demanded the question at the well, whether such a person, by name, be living, in health, sick, or dead? If the party be living and in health, the still quiet water of the well-pit, as soon as the question is demanded, will instantly bubble or boil up as a pot, clear crystalline water; if sick, foul and puddled waters. If the party be dead, it will neither bubble, boil up, nor alter its colour or still motion. However, I can speak nothing of the truth of those supernatural facts from my own sight or experience; but write from the mouths of those who told me they had seen and proved the verity thereof. Finally, it is a strong and courageous fountain of water, kept neat and clean by an old woman of the vicinity, to accommodate strangers for her own advantage, by blazing the virtues and divine qualities of these waters.'[1]

Borlase, writing in 1749, spake of this old dame as lately dead. She seems to have known all the mystic endowments of the fountain, and to have been for a long time its high priestess and dispenser of its virtues. Among its other powers it could reveal the whereabouts of stolen goods, or lost cattle. In Lysons' time the belief in it still held its ground. The spring is called *Gulf-well*, 'the Hebrew brook'.

A chapel or oratory is stated to have once stood in the moor near the well, but no vestiges remain.

This parish is dedicated to St. Gudwall, a British saint, who lived here in the sixth century, and became, according to an ancient calendar, Bishop of St. Malo."—T. Q. C.

It is difficult to find any reliable information with regard to this saint. The Rev. S. Baring-Gould gives the following account of him, but admits that the authorities are not altogether to be depended upon :—

" St. Gudwall was born in Wales, where he was educated and ordained priest and afterwards bishop, but retired from an active life into a cave by the sea-side, with one disciple. His rock was an island, and when the winter storms beat the

[1] " Hals collected materials for a parochial history of Cornwall for half a century, bringing it down to A.D. 1736. Borlase's *Antiquities of Cornwall*, date A.D. 1754, and his *Natural History*, 1758, Queres the same old dame."—T. Q. C.

Atlantic into fury, the foam rushed into the opening of his retreat, and threatened to overwhelm the rock. The legend says that St. Gudwall prayed to God to throw up a barrier against the billows; and the fish came in multitudes with grains of sand in their mouths, and deposited them in one place, till they had reared a long bank, which proved an effectual breakwater. But after a while, when many monks assembled under his direction, he found the place too strait for him; and he built seven boats, placed his monks in them, and led the way, walking on the waters over the Bristol Channel to the coast of Cornwall, and settled at the place named after him, Gulwall, near Penzance. Many stories were told of the saint; amongst others, that he pulled a thorn out of the foot of a wolf that came to him to be healed. The relics of St. Gudwall were translated to Ghent, and preserved in the monastery of Blandinbergh. But others are said to be at Yèvre-le-Chatel, near Pluviers; but it is more probable that these belong to his namesake, the Bishop of Aleth."

The field in which the well was formerly to be seen was a grass field, south of the church; the stream remained for some time after the building had disappeared, but the plough has lately entirely destroyed that also.

GUNWALLOE WELL.

"Nestling for shelter behind a hill in Gunwalloe cove is the miniature church, with its detached tower, dedicated to St. Winolaus, or, as he is here named, St. Gunwalloe, a holy man, who died on the 3rd March, A.D. 529, as is piously recorded in episcopal registers and other documents.[1]

He was a Welshman of noble extraction, and sometime abbot of Landevenick in Brittany. Living before the age of reliable record, we know little of him; but it is singular that he is connected by dedication with this church, and that of the neighbouring parish of Landewednack, which latter circumstance has some suggestions respecting his Armorican abbacy. It is also remarkable that the yearly feast of the two parishes was held on the 3rd March.

The well is close to the church porch, and only a few feet over the precipitous rock which in part forms a breakwater and protection from the waves of the sea. The spring that once bubbled up in its rocky basin is no longer there; sand and stones fill up the well at each high tide, and, though oc-

[1] Oliver's *Monasticon Exon.*, 439. Cumming's *Churches and Antiquities of Cury and Gunwalloe*, p. 183.

casionally cleaned out for the satisfaction of the wayfarer's curiosity, it is only an imperfect semblance of its former self.[1]

That this well was once considered by the country folk of some importance is plain, for one day in the year, called *Gunwalloe day*, was set apart for cleaning out the holy well, a ceremony attended with much festive merriment. This festival, which differed in date from the parish feast, has been discontinued for many years, and lives only in the memories of two of the oldest men in the parish."—T. Q. C.

In 1891 we visited Gunwalloe, and searched long and carefully for the well, but not a trace could we find, the spring even having quite disappeared. The vicar told us that Gunwalloe day is still kept up, but that nothing is now thought of the holy well in connection with it. It is so long since the ceremony of cleaning it out has been gone through, that no recollection of it now exists.

[1] Cumming, *Churches and Antiquities*, p. 182.

ST. GURON'S WELL, BODMIN.

"Near the western doorway of St. Petroc s Church is a plain oblong little building, with a highly pitched roof, and a doorway with a Tudor heading in the southern gable. It was originally built of granite slabs throughout, but has in later times been patched by the insertion of masonry of local stone. The present structure is not of great age, perhaps of sixteenth century date, and contemporary with the two monstrous gurgoyles at the issue below, over which is carved A.D. 1545. Another inscription over the shutes is A.D. 1545.

The water of St. Guron's Well is not now poured out at the ancient outlet, which is about seven feet below the surface of the churchyard ; but, collecting, runs never failingly through the mouths of two hideous heads, one horned, the other with pendent ears. The situation of the spring, flowing from a churchyard, has given the water much undeserved reproach. Carew writes that their conduit water 'runneth thorow the churchyard, the ordinary place of buriall for towne and parish. It breedeth therefore little cause of marvaile that every generall infection is here first admitted and last excluded.'

This prejudice has done much to limit, especially among strangers, the use of this spring of excellent water. It now comes through glazed pottery pipes from a great depth, and interments in the churchyard have long been discontinued.

Night and day, in the driest and hottest seasons, ever flowing, it serves the people with crystal water; a side trough refreshes the passing cattle; and it lays the dust of Bodmin streets; it rolls on, with the Priory rivulet, through the valley, past Scarlet's Well, to pay its tribute to the Camel at Dunmeer.

Looking into the misty past, about the middle of the sixth century of Christ's birth, we see dimly a saintly man, Guron by name, pushing his way, the first Christian missionary to these parts, and settling at Bodmin. The place was then, probably, a deep-wooded glen, through which a constant rivulet ran, surrounded by trackless moors. Here rude Britons dwelt, and fed their cattle on the broad moorlands; part venatic, part pastoral, in their habits; heathen, nearly naked, and savage.

St. Guron settled down among these wild Celts, unarmed except by the weapons of faith, and the example of a sober, religious, and useful life, assisted possibly by some of the leech's cunning.

He soon commended himself to the rude inhabitants of the valley, and gradually taught them the precepts of Christianity. After a few years he was joined by another holy man, St. Petroc, who watered the seed thus sown, and from the small beginnings of this simple hermit's cell, lived to found a religious house, which grew to be, later, a priory of Augústinian monks, St. Guron resigning his missionary charge to the new-comer. If we may judge

St. Guron's Well.

from all that is left us of this age before records, the pioneer St. Guron started in search of a fresh field of labour, and found it at Gorran (St. Guron), on the southern coast of Cornwall.

We know enough of the simple lives of these early apostles to show that in their choice of a spot for settlement they generally pitched their tents, or built their hut, or digged their cell near a constant spring of water,—one of the primary necessaries of even the most ascetic of lives. It is no great stretch of fancy to think that the good Guron fixed his dwelling by this perennial spring, then welling forth from rocks, under shelter, leafy and umbrageous, and still flowing, with different surroundings, to this day.

This well has lost all story among the folk of Bodmin, and it is without any attributive virtue, except as healthful water for common use; which is simply explained by the fact that a church, having some Norman relics within and about it, has been built, and repaired, and restored, several times since St. Guron's days."—T. Q. C.

This well has recently been restored; the accompanying illustration is from a photograph taken in 1891.

HOLY WELL, HALWELL, TREFRY'S.

Harvey writes:—"Halwell, in Robert Reed's part, is a noted consecrated holy well, from which the close had its name. On the north-east corner of Lower Halwell is the chapel-yard of a chapel once there standing; the place where it stood and the ruins of it are yet to be seen. There was also a chapel-house stood there; and the family of the great Lord Trefry did marry, baptise, and bury there, keeping a chaplain in the house. This chapel stood within the space of a hundred feet of the aforesaid holy well, the water of which did then run into the said chapel-yard, and the well is still enclosed with a stone wall all the way from the said chapel-yard, to keep the beasts from defiling and spoiling the said water. This chapel was about a quarter of a mile from the barton-house."

The well is now (1891) in a most dilapidated state, partly held together by the roots of an old tree. Some masonry is lying about; but the old chapel has disappeared, and the stone wall all the way from the well to the said chapel-yard is gone. No tradition relating to it could we discover, nor to whom it was dedicated.

HELSTONE HOLY WELL.

This beautiful little well stands in the corner of a field belonging to Trelill farm, but a short walk from Helstone. It is a fair-sized building of large granite blocks, with a pointed roof, the interior of which is arched on either side, the actual top being composed of two large granite slabs. A rounded arch, five feet seven inches high, and three feet two inches wide, forms the entrance, and on either side of the interior is a rude granite slab, forming a seat. At the back of the interior is another and a smaller arch, measuring three feet seven inches in height, with a width of twenty-one inches; this forms a recess of thirty inches overarching the actual well, the water of which is deep and clear; the larger building being dry, and paved with stone. A square niche is in the wall over this smaller arch, and the building has the appearance of a small well, opening out of a miniature chapel. Ferns grow here and there in the interior, and the roof is overshadowed by a large ivy tree. The full width of the front of the building is seven feet nine inches. There are two rough square niches on either side of the back, and two three-cornered holes over the entrance; but these may be simply the effect of time.

This well resembles, according to many accounts, St. Ruan's Well, Ruan, before its restoration. In Helstone its fame seems to be almost entirely forgotten; but one woman, on being questioned, well remembered visiting the spot in her girlhood for the purpose of dropping a pin accompanied by a wish into its magic waters; she also spoke of a tradition which explained the presence of the building, *viz.*: Many years ago Wendron Church was being built upon the spot; but for some reason, unknown in the present day, there were strong objections to this locality, and crows came by night and removed every stone, with the exception of the porch, which remaining portion now forms the covering of the well.

ST. INGONGAR'S WELL, LANIVET.

Lysons states: "At St. Congar, in this parish, said to have been in ancient times the residence of a hermit, was a chapel and well, dedicated to that Saint".

On reaching St. Ingongar,—as the farm-place is now called,—and inquiring at a cottage for directions to the well, we found that it was quite unknown; and on going to the farm, the servants showed the same want of knowledge of its whereabouts. From this we gathered that it must have fallen entirely, or almost entirely, into disuse and decay. The owner of the farm, however, was able to guide us to it; in fact, it is only about a couple of hundred yards from the house, and might easily be passed as a gutter or drain. When we saw it (July, 1891) it was dry, but there is water in it sometimes; its appearance is that of a drain under a trodden way, leading up to a gap in the hedge. The sides are of stone, but evidently modern; the top seems to be composed of one large stone covered with well-trodden earth, and in the hedge close by is the decayed trunk of a felled tree, which must at one time have overshadowed the well.

No traditions concerning it can we discover; the

water is rarely used, certainly not for any particular purposes; and the fact of those people living within a few yards of it and knowing nothing of its existence, shows that it is not held in any esteem.

No traces of a chapel are to be seen near. The owner of the farm thought that the working of some machinery on the other side of the hedge may have been to some extent the cause of the draining of the well.

Whitaker suggests that St. Wingel, the mother of St. Piran, may have been the patron saint of this well. She came over from Ireland, and settled not far from her son, with the nuns who had accompanied her. Lanivet, in which parish St. Ingongar is situated, is only about twenty miles from Perranzabuloe. This idea may possibly be a correct, though not a very probable, one.

JESUS WELL, ST. MINVER.

"This rude well stands on a bleak high down, in the lowlands of St. Minver, where water could hardly be expected. The spot is so bare, and exposed to the storms which devastate this coast,

that it is often half buried with the drifted sea-sand from the beaches near. The building is square in form, with a highly pitched but truncated roof of masonry. A niche of rude shape is in the further end of the well; it may be to hold a drinking vessel, a crucifix, or effigy of saint.

The people of the place tell some story giving a miraculous origin to this fairly constant stream. Some pilgrim saint travelling over this sandy dune, wearied and thirsty, struck the arid soil with his staff (as Moses smote the rock in Horeb), and the water came out abundantly. Some faith in the extraordinary healthful quality of the water still remains among the country folk. I was shown this well by old 'Fiddler Thomas,' of Brayhill, an odd character, well known to all visitors by his curious collection of remains of animal life, some of them of extinct species, his old coins, and other ancient things picked out of the drifting sandhills; and also by his long-winded disquisitions when on this his favourite trail."[1]—T. Q. C.

Maclean, in his *History of Trigg Minor*, speaks of the old chapel, Jesus Chapel, which formerly stood not far from the well. "Upon the manor of Penmayne, about half a mile north of Rock, on the left of the road leading to St. Minver Church, is an ancient enclosed tenement, containing about four acres, called 'Chapel'. A small chapel existed here until recent times. Mr. Sandys, writing in 1812, states that he had seen pieces of a Gothic window on the spot; but no remains are now to be found. . . . Near the above-mentioned

[1] On inquiry we learned that "Fiddler Thomas" had been dead some time, and his museum disposed of.

chapel, in a north-west direction, is an ancient holy well, called Jesus Well. It possessed a fine spring, the waters of which were believed to have great healing qualities. People came from long distances to pay their devotions and use the waters, which were celebrated for many cures, and for the evils which befell scoffing unbelievers. Its virtues continued till late years. No longer ago than 1867, Mary Cranwell (the wife of a boatman named Patrick Cranwell, since deceased), who for a considerable period had suffered severely from erysipelas, and could obtain no relief from medical treatment, fully believing, as she stated to the author, from the repute of the well, that if she bathed in the water with faith she would be cured of her disease, went to the place, and kneeling beside the well recited the 'Litany to the Holy Name of Jesus,' and bathed the diseased parts in the waters. She received relief from the first application; and repeating it the prescribed number of three times, at intervals, she became perfectly whole, and has never since suffered from the same malady. Whether this remarkable cure, which as a fact is fully verified, arose from any curative qualities in the waters, or was the result of the poor woman's faith, we will not venture to say. Unfortunately, the properties of the waters cannot now be tested, inasmuch as the farmer who occupies the land, not knowing, or probably not believing in, its virtues, has, since the above-mentioned circumstance, cut a drain to the spring, and intercepted the flow of water. There is a small building of some antiquity over the well, having a doorway with a two-centred arch, consisting of three stones, but it is now much out of repair."

Whether the above-mentioned farmer relented and became a believer in the virtues of Jesus Well, or whether his drainage system was faulty, we know not; but there is certainly plenty of water there at present, and on inquiry we found that children suffering from whooping-cough are still taken to drink of it. An old man whom we met near by, told us that he could remember the time when children were passed through the waters, or dipped, for whooping-cough, also when pins were dropped in for the telling of fortunes, and even money was cast into its depths for the same reason; and he mentioned one particular Sunday on which he had seen as much as sixteen shillings taken out by unbelievers, who thus reaped the benefit of the superstitions of others; this fortune-telling has quite ceased. The well has fallen somewhat to decay during the last ten or twenty years; the archway has disappeared, as has also the front part of the roof, otherwise it looks much the same. Cattle were in the field in which the well stands, and had trampled down the ground around the building. It is about five feet square, and the interior is lined with beautiful ferns.

JETWELLS HOLY WELL.

Sir John Maclean, in his *History of Trigg Minor* (vol. i, p. 346), says:—"Jetwells contains about eighteen acres of rich meadow land. It derives its name from a holy well which formerly existed on the premises, and which has been ruthlessly torn down, and the place desecrated within the last twenty years. The abundant spring is still known by the name of 'The Holy Well'."

The two stones which formed the ancient equilateral arch still lie on the spot, as also do other stones which formed the building. In early times the tenement was called "St. Gitwell Parks," which is a corruption or abbreviation of "St. Julitta's Well Parks". In 1569 it is mentioned under the name of "St. Gitwill Park".

On 30th June, 1891, we visited Jetwells Holy Well, as it is now called, expecting to find simply the uncovered spring, as the *Parochial History of Cornwall* stated that, "in one of the fields stood an ancient holy well which gave name to the place; it was thoughtlessly destroyed within the last twenty years, and the materials used in the inferior out-buildings of the premises". We were therefore much surprised to see a well-preserved little structure, looking as if it had stood there unmolested for scores of years.

Thanks to the kindness of the owner of Jetwells house, whose property it now is, we were permitted to see and photograph it;[1] and from her we learnt that many years ago it had been destroyed as stated, but her husband, the late Colonel S. Bake, when he repurchased the estate, had the stones collected and replaced over the spring. That this restoration has taken place seems to be almost entirely unknown even now, as an old woman in Lanteglos informed us, when we inquired about the well, that although she had lived in the parish so long, and had worked on the estate for years, she had never seen it,—though she had heard of Jetwells Holy Well,—and she assured us there was no building whatever to photograph; we were also so assured in Camelford.

The well is situated in a hollow near the bottom of a field,—a quaint, picturesque, little structure, with a weather-beaten thorn growing on a ledge above it, and luxuriant ferns lining the interior. The roof, which slopes back to the level of the field, is rounded, and composed of rough masonry; the doorway is arched, the stone being evidently the original one; there is an old stone step at the entrance, slightly guttered in the middle; but the copious spring no longer runs over it—overflowing

1 The plate was unfortunately destroyed after we had left the county.—Eds.

the building and the surrounding field as in former times—for the superfluous water is now drained off in one channel underground, and flows into a miniature lake at the bottom of the field.

We could hear of no tradition connected with the well, nor that its water was ever used for any special purpose.

With regard to the saint there is very little known. There is, of course, the St. Julitta, who suffered persecution at Cæsarea, in Cappadocia, in 303; but one can hardly connect her with a church and parish in an out-of-the-way spot in Cornwall.

Sir John Maclean gives what seems by far the most reasonable explanation, in his *History of Trigg Minor*:—

"The Celtic form of Julitta is 'Ilid,' and there was a daughter of Brechan named 'Ilud,' whose designation in Latin would also be *Julitta*. As a group of Brechan's numerous children settled on the north coast of Cornwall, and founded several of the churches in this deanery, it becomes a question whether St. Julitta of Lanteglos may not be identical with her."

ST. JOHN'S WELL, MORWENSTOW.

Not far from the church, and by the side of a back drive leading to the Vicarage, is St. John's Well, still in very good condition; a substantial little building covers it, on the pointed roof of

St. John's Well, Morwenstow.

which is a cross, and a wooden door guards the entrance. The water is particularly cool and pure, and during Mr. Hawker's time in Morwenstow, as vicar of the parish, he would never drink any other, and always had it used in the font for baptisms; this custom is, I believe, still continued. There was once a lawsuit to decide the ownership of St. John's Well. Sir J. Buller, afterwards Lord Churston, claimed it for his own, which claim the vicar (Mr. Hawker) strongly opposed; and the law allowed him his right. The lines written by him on the subject of his well may not be inappropriate here.

"They dream'd not in old Hebron, when the sound
Went through the city, that the promised Son
Was born to Zachary, and his name was John—
They little thought that here, in this far ground,
Beside the Severn Sea, that Hebrew child
Would be a cherish'd memory of the Wild!
Here, where the pulses of the Ocean bound
Whole centuries away,—while one meek Cell,
Built by the Fathers o'er a lonely Well,
Still breathes the Baptist's sweet remembrance round!
A Spring of silent waters, with his name
That from the Angel's voice in music came,
Here in the wilderness so faithful found,
It freshens to this day the Levite's grassy mound."

ST. JULIAN'S WELL, MOUNT EDGCUMBE.

This well, which had become very ruinous, was restored in the year 1882 by its noble owner and careful guardian, the Earl of Mount Edgcumbe, under the guidance of that excellent architect Mr.

ST. JULIAN'S (SECTION).

James Hine, F.R.I.B.A., who gives this account of it.

"Probably the most ancient example of that curious and to some extent unexplained class of buildings, the Cornish well-chapel, is that of St.

Julian's at Mount Edgcumbe. It is very small, its internal dimensions being only six feet three inches by four feet nine inches, and it was vaulted over by an equilateral stone arch formed by level bedded courses of masonry with a central chamfered rib resting on moulded corbels. The doorway, or rather gateway (because there was no

St. Julian's.

door), at the entrance end had also a pointed arch springing from the same line as that of the vault. The proportions are as simple as they are beautiful, and the details and character of the masonry fix the period approximately as that of the early part of the fourteenth century.

"It appears not to have been thought essential that these well-chapels should stand east and west, like our parish churches; and whilst the one at St. Cleather follows that position, this little building is placed north and south. At the southern or fountain end is a niche which probably contained a figure of the patron saint. In the western side-wall, near the fountain, is another and lower recess, with an ogee chamfered arch corresponding with the other. The jambs, existing, of the door-way, the rib and corbels of the roof, as well as the niches, are of a green freestone from the parish of Landrake; the rest of the masonry is of more local stone. The pavement was of red and green glazed tiles, fragments of which we have found."

Of its patron saint little or nothing can be said with certainty. Whether she was the St. Juliana, one of Brechan's family, who is considered the possible patron and founder of Maker Church, in which parish the well stands, or St. Julian, who in all mediæval mythology is represented as being fated to kill his parents, is open to conjecture; but the former seems the more probable. Whichever it was, he or she does not seem to have endowed the spring with any peculiar virtues, or to have left legend or history behind.

ST. JULIOT'S WELL.

Polsue, writing of the parish of St. Juliot, says:—"Of the patron saint of this church, St. Juliot, Julyot, Julitta, or Juletta, very little is known. She is said to have suffered death, having been accused by a violent and wicked person who had previously taken from her by force some large possessions. There is extant a sermon of St. Basil in praise of this saint, who is commemorated in the ancient Roman Calendar on the 30th of July." The holy well of this saint is said to have been situated in a field which borders Hennett marsh, and a few yards to the right of the road which leads from St. Juliot Church to Anderton; about thirty years ago it was filled in, on account of its being dangerous to cattle. There were at one time some curiously carved stones surrounding the well, one representing the figure, it was supposed, of the Virgin Mary; but they were—perhaps with some feeling of reverence for them—buried either in the well or near the site. The country folk have it that pilgrims used to visit St. Juliot's Well, and use its waters for the cure of skin diseases. Rather more than thirty years ago, when Hennett marsh was being drained, one of the labourers found a gold circlet, said to have been worn on the head, and lost by a pilgrim (perhaps it was an offering left behind); this circlet was sold to a local antiquarian for its weight in sovereigns, who afterwards re-sold it to an editor of a well-known daily newspaper, who finally, it is said, presented it to the British Museum.

WELL IN KENWYN CHURCHYARD.

This well, near the south door of Kenwyn Churchyard, is very uncommon in appearance, but has no traditions or virtues attached to it.

At the bottom of a flight of narrow stone steps is an arched doorway, within which is the spring. The little building covering it has evidently been somewhat lately restored; for the arched doorway is of bricks in very good condition, as are also the back, and one side, at least. The walls on either side of the steps are of stone with no mortar, and an old granite curbing runs round the top. This well is said to be much older than the church.

HOLY WELL, ST. KEW.

The history of the saint who gave his name to the parish of St. Kew seems to be hidden in obscurity: even when and whence he came is quite unrecorded. The parish was not always known as St. Kew; its more ancient name being Lanow, or sometimes Lanow Seynt. The holy well is situated by the front gate of the vicarage. Many years ago when the old house was pulled down the road was diverted, and in the alterations made at the time the well was buried and lost sight of altogether. The present vicar (Rev. N. T. Every), on learning from an old clergyman of the parish what (to this old gentleman's great disgust and anger) had been done, set to work to unearth the holy well once again, and at length found it; he caused it to be arched over, and placed a cross on the top; he also planted it about with trees and shrubs, and still has all the water for drinking purposes fetched from it. The old clergyman, and also an old inhabitant of the parish, affirmed that the quality of the water used to be thought very highly of, and people came purposely to drink of it. The present vicar is to be greatly commended for the trouble and expense he was at in causing the restoration of this parish holy well.

THE WELL OF ST. KEYNE.

ST. KEYNE.

About half a mile east of the church of St. Keyne, and pleasantly situated in a deep valley, is this celebrated spring. There is nothing architecturally interesting in the building enclosing it; but it is remarkable for the variety of trees which grow in such crowded space upon its roof, and more especially for the power with which its water has for ages been popularly gifted.

"Next," says Carew, "I will relate you another of the Cornish natural wonders, *viz.*, St. Kayne's Well; but lest you make a wonder first at the saint, before you take notice of the well, you must understand that this was not Keyne, the man-queller, but one of a gentler spirit, and milder sex, —to wit, a woman. He who caused the spring to be pictured added this rhyme for an exposition:—

"'In name, in shape, in quality
This well is very quaint;
The name to lot of Kayne befell,
No over holy saint.

"'The shape four trees of divers kind,
Withy, oak, elm, and ash,
Make with their roots an arched roof
Whose floor this spring doth wash.

"'The quality, that man or wife,
Whose chance, or choice, attains,
First of the sacred stream to drink,
Thereby the mastery gains.'"

St. Keyne, who lived towards the end of the fifth century, was one of the fifteen children (out of the twenty-six of whom St. Brechan was the happy father) who were sainted, and of those fifteen she stands out as the most saintly and most beautiful in mind and body.[1] Though of surpassing loveliness, she wandered about the country, safe from insult or wrong by "the strength of her purity," performing most astonishing miracles in all parts.

The name of Keynsham is given to that part of Somerset because of the miracle St. Keyne worked there, namely, changing all the serpents, with which the spot was infested, into stone.

After a long life spent in doing good in various parts of the country, she retired to Cornwall and made her home in the beautiful valley, and not far from the well, which bears her name. Over the well she planted an oak, an ash, an elm, and a withy, and blessed them. But it was not until her death that she endowed the waters with their peculiar virtue. When dying she was carried to the well on a litter, and, soothed by the mur-

[1] In the young women's window in St. Neot's Church, St. Brechan is represented, and in the folds of his robe are the portraits of his fifteen sainted children.

mur and ripple of the stream, she blessed it, "desiring above all things," says Hunt, "peace on earth; and she hoped to benefit the world, by giving to woman a chance of being equal to her lord and master".

Southey has these verses on it:—

"A well there is in the west-country,
And a clearer one never was seen,
There is not a wife in the west-country,
But has heard of the Well of St. Keyne.

"An oak and an elm tree stand beside,
And behind does an ash tree grow;
And a willow from the bank above
Droops to the water below.

"A traveller came to the Well of St. Keyne,
Joyfully he drew nigh,
For from cock-crow he had been travelling,
And there was not a cloud in the sky.

"He drank of the water so cool and clear,
For thirsty and hot was he,
And he sat down upon the bank
Under the willow tree.

"There came a man from the house hard by
At the well to fill his pail;
On the well-side he rested it,
And he bade the stranger hail.

"'Now art thou a bachelor, stranger?' quoth he,
'For an if thou hast a wife,
The happiest draught thou hast drank this day
That ever thou didst in thy life.

"'Or has thy good woman, if one thou hast,
  Ever here in Cornwall been?
For an if she have, I'll venture my life
  She has drank of the Well of St. Keyne.'

"'I have left a good woman who never was here,'
  The stranger he made reply;
'But that my draught should be the better for that,
  I pray you answer me why.'

"'St. Keyne,' quoth the Cornishman, 'many a time
  Drank of this crystal well;
And before the Angel summon'd her,
  She laid on the water a spell.

"'If the Husband of this gifted well
  Shall drink before his Wife,
A happy man thenceforth is he,
  For he shall be Master for life.

"'But if the Wife should drink of it first,
  God help the Husband then!'
The stranger stoopt to the Well of St. Keyne
  And drank of the water again.

"'You drank of the well I warrant betimes?'
  He to the Cornishman said,
But the Cornishman smiled as the stranger spake,
  And sheepishly shook his head.

"'I hasten'd as soon as the wedding was done,
  And left my Wife in the porch;
But, i' faith, she had been wiser than me,
  For she took a bottle to Church.'"

"These verses are erroneously said to have been suggested to the Laureate while he was on a visit to the Rev. William Farwell, the Rector of St.

Martin's by Looe. Mr. Bond, the historian of the Looes, has reprinted them in his book, published in the year 1823, and he there states that the ballad had then 'appeared a few years since'. He makes no mention of Southey's visit, and I find that the Rev. Dr. Michell was rector at the time, Farwell having been admitted as lately as 1830.

Bond sent a sketch of the well and its trees to Sylvanus Urban, and it was inserted in the *Gentleman's Magazine* for 1799.[1] Another ballad about it is to be found in this venerable serial for June, 1822.[2]

The trees are not as they were in the time of Carew and Norden. The oak, elm, and withy were blown down in a very fierce storm which occurred in the November of 1703. Some years afterwards, Mr. Rashleigh of Menabilly planted the present trees in their place, five in number, —two oak, two ash, and an elm; and it is a double wonder, firstly, where in such a scant place they get nourishment; secondly, why by their roots they do not disrupt the masonry, and ruin the well. When standing on the top of the well, all the trunks could be reached by the extended arms.

On my last visit, one of the oaks was much decayed, and supported by a prop.

[1] Vol. lxix, pp. 192-4.

[2] Vol. xcii, p. 546. Pictures of this well are also to be found in Blight's *Cornish Crosses*.

The well has now no architectural interest, the entrance being a plain round-headed arch of native stone.

The curious endowment of this spring is shared by a strange chair-shaped excavation, or fracture, in the outer side of a tall pinnacle on a tower, a portion of the structure which so appropriately crowns St. Michael's Mount in Cornwall. The person who has nerve enough to sit in this chair at such a giddy height, with his legs dangling over the abyss beneath, is well fitted for the mastery, and richly deserves it. It is said that ladies have been known to dare the danger of this exploit, for the guerdon, and I was told by an eye-witness that a man, laying hold of the masonry, vaulted into the chair and returned safely from his foolhardy enterprise.

It has been related that Mr. Leah, then rector of the parish of St. Keyne, sent two dozen bottles of this gifted well water to a bazaar in the grounds of Mount Edgcumbe, and that they met with a ready sale at two shillings a bottle, with a loud demand for more." —T. Q. C.

On visiting the well in 1891, we found it in a very dilapidated state, the arch tumbling to pieces. Of the five trees only two are left, an elm and an ash, both fine trees, particularly the elm.

LADY'S WELL, MEVAGISSEY.

This well was doubtless one of those dedicated in former days to the Blessed Virgin; the name changing as time went on from "Our Lady's Well," to "My Lady's Well," and latterly to "Lady's Well". It is situated about a quarter of a mile from Mevagissey, on the manor of Trelevan, and the water, which gushes out from a rock at the foot of a steep hill, has never been known to fail. The well was said to possess great healing powers, and also to have the property of giving increased vigour and strength to the constitution. It was formerly held in great veneration, and has been frequently resorted to, by persons in search of health and strength, within living memory.

LADY'S WELL, PADSTOW.

This well, "The Well of Our Lady," has entirely disappeared.

LANEAST WELL.

"Is in a secluded glen, a short distance from the church. It is called by some of the people around the 'Wishing Well,' by others the 'Jordan'. The building is six feet eight inches long, and six feet in width; the entrance, by a round-headed arch, is on the south. The water from this excellent spring was, and probably still is, used for several rites. It is somewhat strange that two of the clergy of the parish in succession can give me no information about the well, though near their very doors; but I find an anonymous writer, whose reverence is to be commended, plaintively writing in a local newspaper thus: 'If the attention of the Penzance Antiquarian Society were directed to the state of the holy well at Laneast, and the remains of the old Chapel Park, St. Clether, they might perhaps induce the proprietors of these remnants of antiquity to bestow a little care on the same, and arrest their further ruin and destruction'.

I fear that Blight's drawing and brief note will be soon all that remains of it. After much inquiry I can find that the 'Wishing Well' is still consulted for intimations of the future; but the time and mode of invocation I have not been able to discover. I have asked of two vicars of the parish about the well, and they were vaguely aware of its existence."—T. Q. C.

LANEAST HOLY WELL, 1891.

This lack of interest seems to continue; for a letter to the vicar inquiring as to the present condition of the well, and in what esteem it is now held, received no reply; but on visiting it we were fortunate enough to meet with an intelligent old woman who guided us to the spot where the well stands in a marshy field on the opposite side of the road to the church. She had cleaned the church for many years, and in former times used to fetch the water for baptisms from this well, but the custom is discontinued now; she also remembers the time when all the villagers went to it to make their butter; but of its use as a *wishing* well she had no recollection, and seemed unaware that it had ever been used for that purpose.

The building is now in very fair condition, but perfectly plain and unadorned; it is picturesquely situated, with a large elder tree overshadowing the roof on one side, the other being covered with ferns, while before the door, which is an ordinary wooden one with an iron clasp, stands a tall ash tree, surrounded by brambles, rushes and a profusion of forget-me-nots. The little well is quite unapproachable, at least such was the case in 1891, owing to the marshy nature of the ground, but perhaps the unusually wet weather of that year was the cause of it.

ST. LEVAN'S WELL.

"One whose pen has done much to rescue from oblivion the fast falling antiquities of his native

county writes thus of St. Levan's Well:[1] 'Standing on some elevated rocks on Porthchapel Point,

[1] Blight's *Week at the Land's End*, p. 131.

the remains of St. Levan's Well are seen in a little glen beneath. Still, no sign of life, a deep solitude hangs around the great cliffs; the babbling of a little stream over its rough bed, blended with the murmurs of the waves below, is the only sound that breaks on the ear. This was the spot chosen by St. Levan for his chapel or hermitage, which stood on the verge of the cliffs; the well was farther back, but steps communicated from one to the other; these, however, have disappeared. The site of the chapel can only be guessed at, whilst the walls of the little baptistery are wildly overgrown by rushes and tall water-plants. Thus is the altar overthrown, the shrine deserted, and the place become a wilderness.'

Tradition says that St. Levan spent some of his time at Bodillan, about three-quarters of a mile distant; and the path thence through Rose-pletha which he took to go to Pedn-mên-an-mere, the 'stone head-land by the sea,' to fish, is still visible, being marked by a stronger vegetation. It is also said of him, as of St. Neot (probably the persons are confounded), that he caught only one fish a day, which served for his sustenance. Whilst thus dwelling in seclusion, he was surprised by an unexpected visit from his sister and her child. To entertain them, he proceeded to his fishing station, threw out the line, and presently drew up a fish, a chad. As he had visitors, this was not considered dainty enough, so it was thrown back into the water again. A second time was the line cast forth, and behold the same fish was caught. It was again thrown into the sea. And now the saint changed his position to another rock, and threw the line still farther out. Lo! what was his surprise when the same fish again presented itself! Then the saint thought that the hand of Providence was concerned in the matter, and he bare his catch away. It was cooked, and placed before the guests; but, sad to relate, the child was choked by the first mouthful. Then was the holy man much grieved, and repented that he had given way to the temptation of the fish, which, he now doubted not, was possessed by an evil spirit; yet he believed, if he had been content with it at the first time, the melancholy accident would not have happened, but that it was a punishment for his dissatisfaction in not accepting gratefully what Providence had appointed him. From that time the fishermen have called the chad *chuck-cheeld*, *i.e.*, choke-child."—T. Q. C.

At the present time there is no pool or depression of any kind; but that there is a spring is shown by the swampy nature of the ground around. The well, which is in an enclosure, about three feet in length and breadth, is surrounded by a wall, against one side of which the earth has accumulated, giving the structure the appearance of a hillock, at a distance. Scattered about, and half embedded in the grass, are a lot of roughly hewn stones, evidently the remains of some building, the character of which is not known. The well is most romantically situated, but is very difficult to get at, and is now never used. Lower down the cliff is the oratory of St. Levan.

ST. LUDGVAN'S WELL.

In his *Romances of the West of England* Hunt tells the legend of St. Ludgvan as follows: "St. Ludgvan, an Irish missionary, had finished his work. On the hill-top, looking over the most beautiful of bays, the church stood with all its blessings. Yet the saint, knowing human nature, determined on associating with it some object of a miraculous character, which should draw people from all parts of the world to Ludgvan. The saint prayed over the dry earth, which was beneath him, as he knelt on the church stile. His prayer was for water, and presently a most beautiful crystal stream welled up from below. The holy man prayed on, and then, to try the virtues of the water, he washed his eyes. They were rendered at once more powerful, so penetrating, indeed, as to enable him to see microscopic objects. The saint prayed again, and then he drank of the water. He discovered that his powers of utterance were greatly improved, his tongue formed words with scarcely any effort of his will. The saint now prayed that all children baptised in the waters of this well might be protected against the hangman and his hempen cord; and an angel from heaven came down into the water, and promised the saint that his prayers should be granted. Not long after this, a good farmer and his wife brought their babe to the saint, that it might derive all the blessings belonging to this holy well. The priest stood at the baptismal font, the parents with their friends around. The saint proceeded with the baptismal ceremonial, and at length the time arrived when he took the tender babe into his holy arms. He signed the sign of the cross over the child, and when he sprinkled water on the face of the infant its face glowed with a divine intelligence. The priest then proceeded with the prayer; but, to the astonishment of all, whenever he used the name of Jesus, the child, who had received the miraculous power of speech from the water, pronounced distinctly the name of the devil, much to the consternation of all present. The saint knew that an evil spirit had taken possession of the child, and he endeavoured to cast him out; but the devil proved stronger than the saint for some time. St. Ludgvan was not to be beaten; he knew that the spirit was a restless soul, which had been exorcised from Treassow, and he exerted all his energies in prayer. At length the spirit became obedient, and left the child. He was now commanded by the saint to take his flight to the Red Sea. He rose, before the terrified spectators, into a gigantic size; he then spat into the well; he laid hold of the pinnacles of the tower, and shook the church until they thought it would fall. The saint was alone unmoved. He prayed on, until, like a flash of lightning, the demon vanished, shaking down a pinnacle in his flight. The demon, by spitting in the water, destroyed the spells of the water upon the eyes and the tongue too: but it fortunately retains its virtue of preventing any child baptised in it from being hanged with a cord of hemp. Upon a cord of silk it is stated to have no power."

Many years after this virtue was bestowed upon St. Ludgvan's Well its reputation was in great jeopardy, for a Ludgvan woman was convicted of murder, and most successfully hanged with a hempen cord. This was a great shock to the faith of the people of Ludgvan, and they began to have horrible misgivings as to their safety and the safety of their children from the hand and hempen rope of the hangman. But after anxious and diligent search in the parish register it was ascertained that this woman had not been baptised in St. Ludgvan Church, and her name was afterwards found in the register of a neighbouring parish. The villagers were filled with joy and relief, and their belief in the powers of the waters of their well was firmer than ever.

In the present day, however, the tradition of its great virtues is but carelessly remembered; the people speak of the water as very good indeed, but nothing more. No building over it now remains, if ever there was one, and the stream is brought down to the village, where it issues through a "shute," and is used by the villagers generally.

MADRON WELL.

"In the near neighbourhood of Penzance, and about three-quarters of a mile from the church and church-town of Madron, the traveller, bearing to the right in a north-easterly direction, through field and marshy moor, will find the celebrated Madron Well.

It is impossible to guess, such are the ravages of fanatic violence and time, as to what the well and baptistery originally were. About thirty years ago I visited it, and it was then in a very ruined state. There was nothing of the shapely and sculptured form of many of our Eastern wells about it. It was merely an oblong space, enclosed by rough old walling, in which were, in the south-west corner, a dilapidated well, with an inlet and outlet for water; a raised row of stones in front of this, and the remains of stone benches.

The accompanying ground plan, copied from Blight, will make this description plainer. 'The length of the building is twenty-five feet, breadth sixteen feet, the walls two feet thick; the altar stone, *A*, is five feet ten inches in length, two feet seven inches wide, and stands two feet ten inches above the level of the floor; *B* is a socket, nine inches by eight, where a cross or the image of the patron saint may have been placed; *C* is a row of stones, forming a step which divides the chancel from the nave; *E*, *E*, the remains of stone benches or seats; *D*, the doorway, which faces exactly north; it is two feet wide without, and two feet eight inches within; in the south-west corner is an excavation, *G*, which appears to have been used as a font, the water being supplied

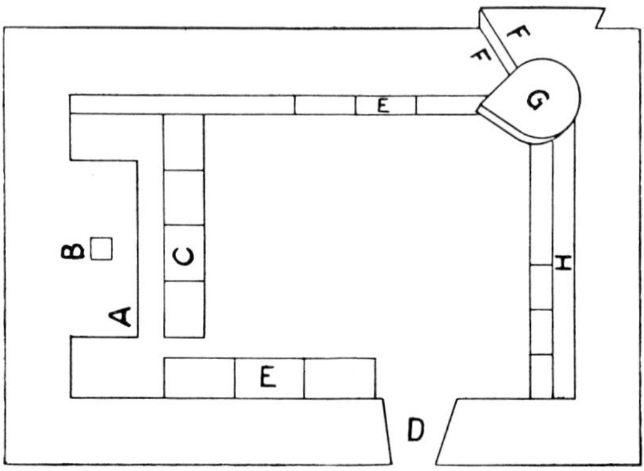

from the well above, for which purpose there is an inlet in the wall at *F*; *H* is a drain to carry off the waste water. The building was enclosed by an outer wall, remains of which may still be seen.'[1]

Many stories have been told by writers of authority of the virtues of this renowned well, with the ordinary quantity, quality of evidence, and authentication. The learned, pious, but unfortu-

[1] Blight's *Ancient Crosses, etc., in the West of Cornwall.*

nate Bishop Hall, then living in the comparative quiet of the see of Exeter, visited this well in the year 1640 or 1641, and thus writes of it in his treatise on *The Invisible World:* —

'The trade we have with good spirits is not now drawn by the eye, but is like to themselves, spiritual; yet not so but that even in bodily occasions we have many times insensible helps from them in such manner, as that, by the effects, we can boldly say, "Here hath been an angel, though we saw him not". Of this kind was that no less than miraculous cure, which at St. Maderne's (S. Maternus), in Cornwall, was wrought on a poor cripple, one John Trelille; whereof, besides the many attestations of many hundreds of the neighbours, I took a strict and personal examination in that last visitation (at Whitsuntide), which I either did or shall hold. This man, that for sixteen years together was fain to walk upon his hands, by reason of the close contraction of the sinews of his limbs, was, upon three monitions in his dream to wash in that well, suddenly so restored to his limbs, that I saw him able both to walk, and to get his own maintenance. I found here neither art nor collusion; the thing done, the Author invisible.'[1]

Another (unknown) writing, a little later, gives a fuller and more circumstantial account of this instance of the miraculous power of the well.

'I will relate one miracle more, done in our own

[1] Book i, section 8.

country, to the great wonder of the inhabitants, but a few years ago, *viz.*, about the year 1640. The process of the business was told the king when at Oxford, which he caused to be further examined.

'It was this: a certain boy of twelve years of age, called John Trelille, in the coast of Cornwall, not far from the Land's End, as they were playing at football, snatching up the ball, ran away with it; whereupon a girl, in anger, struck him with a thick stick on the backbone, and so bruised or broke it that for sixteen years after he was forced to go creeping on the ground. In this condition he arrived to the twenty-eighth year of his age, when he dreamed that if he did but bathe in St. Maderne's Well, or in the stream running from it, he should recover his former strength and health. This is a place in Cornwall frequented at this time by many on the Thursday in May, near to which well is a chapel dedicated to St. Maderne, where is yet an altar, and right against it a grassy hillock (made every year anew by the country people), which they call St. Maderne's bed.

'The chapel roof is quite decayed; but a kind of thorn, of itself shooting forth out of the old walls, so extends its boughs that it covers the whole chapel, and supplies as it were a roof. On Thursday in May, assisted by one Perriman, his neighbour, entertaining great hopes from his dream, thither he crept, and lying before the altar, and praying very fervently that he might regain his health and the strength of his limbs, he washed his whole body in the stream that flowed from the well and ran through the chapel. After which, having slept for one hour and a half in St. Maderne's bed, through the extremity of the pain he felt in his nerves and arteries, he began to cry out, and his companions helping him and lifting him up, he perceived his limbs and joints somewhat expanded, and himself become stronger; insomuch that partly with his hands he went more erect than before. Before the following Thursday he got two crutches, resting on which he would make a shift to walk, which before he could not do; and coming to the chapel as before, after having bathed himself, he slept on the same bed, and awakening, found himself much stronger and more upright; and so, leaving one crutch in the chapel he went home with the other. The third Thursday he returned to the chapel, and bathed as before, slept, and when he awoke rose up quite cured; yea, grew so strong that he wrought day-labour among other hired servants; and four years after listed himself as a soldier in the king's army, where he behaved himself with great stoutness both of mind and body; at length in 1644 he was slain at Lyme in Dorsetshire.'

During the revolutionary troubles and when the Parliamentary faction was in the ascendant, this well is said to have been much damaged by the iconoclastic zeal of a Major Ceely of St. Ives. I have been able to get no proof of this, but only the vaguest rumour in guide-books and elsewhere, which rumour is being strengthened by constant repetition. It has some, but not much, probability, when we compare the condition of the building in 1640, according to the authority last cited,—its roof quite decayed, and its shelter deputed to an old thorn which spread its friendly boughs over the enclosure,—with its condition two centuries later, when weather, age, and neglect had worked their will upon it.

William Scawen, Esq., Vice-Warden of the Stannaries of Cornwall, in a MS. preserved in the Bodleian Library, gives the following story in confirmation of the virtues of the well, and showing that late into the eighteenth century it had lost, at least in popular belief, none of its curative power.

'Of St. Mardren's Well (which is a parish west to the Mount), a fresh true story of two persons, both of them lame and decrepit, thus recovered from their infirmity. These two persons, after they had applied themselves to divers physicians and chirurgeons for cure, and finding no success by them, they resorted to St. Mardren's Well; and according to the ancient custom which they had heard of, the same which was once in a year—to whit, on Corpus Christi evening, to lay some small offering there, and to lie on the ground all night, drink of the water there, and in the morning after to take a good draught more, and to take and carry away some of the water, each of them in a bottle, at their departure. This course these two men followed, and within three weeks they found the effect of it, and by degrees, their strength increasing, were able to move themselves on crutches. The year following they took the same course again, after which they were able to go with the help of a stick; and at length one of them, John Thomas, being a fisherman, was, and is, at this day, able to follow his fishing craft. The other, whose name was William Cork, was a soldier under the command of my kinsman, Colonel William Godolphin (as he has often told me), was able to perform his duty, and died in the service of His Majesty, King Charles. But here-with take also this:—

'One Mr. Hutchins, a person well known in those parts, and now lately dead, being parson of Ludgvan, a near neighbouring parish to St. Mardren's Well, he observed that many of his parishioners often frequented this well superstitiously, for which he reproved them privately, and sometimes publicly in his sermons; but afterwards he, the said Mr. Hutchins, meeting with a woman coming from the well with a bottle in her hand, desired her earnestly that he might drink thereof, being then troubled with cholical pains, which accordingly he did, and was eased of his infirmity. The latter story is a full confutation of the former; for if taking the water accidentally thus prevailed upon the party to his cure, as it is likely it did, then the miracle which was intended to be by the ceremony of lying on the ground and offering, is wholly fled, and it leaves the virtue of the water to be the true cause of the cure. And we have here, as in many places of the land, great variety of salutary springs which have diversity of operations which by natural reason have been found to be productive of good effects, and not by miracle, as the vain fancies of monks and friars have been exercised in heretofore.'[1]

Another writer of later date says that 'here divination is performed on May morning by rustic maidens anxious to know when they are to be married. Two pieces of straw about an inch long are crossed and transfixed with a pin. This, floated on the waters, elicits bubbles, the number of which, carefully counted, denotes the years before the happy day.'[2]

In a pilgrimage which I made to this well in 1845, I observed the custom of hanging rags and bandages on the thorns which grew around. I have not noticed this observance elsewhere in Cornwall. This curious habit of leaving rags or some part of the clothes of the sick and impotent, and even

[1] This notice of Madron Well was printed by Davies Gilbert among the appendices to his *Parochial History of Cornwall*. The complete title is "Observations on an ancient manuscript entitled *Passio Christo*, written in the Cornish language, and now preserved in the Bodleian Library, with an account of the language, manners and customs of the people of Cornwall, from a manuscript in the library of Thomas Artle, Esq., 1777".

[2] Hunt's *Popular Romances and Drolls*.

their crutches, at the sacred well, whether as mementoes of the cure, or the only offerings the grateful, whilome cripple could afford, is very nearly of world-wide range. Hanway, in his *Travels into Persia,*[1] on coming to a desolate caravanserai, where was a spring and a tree, noticed 'a number of rags tied to the branches' of the tree. These were placed there by the travellers coming from Ghilan, a province remarkable for agues, left there in the belief that with the rags they left their diseases behind them.

Even in the interior of Africa, the traveller Park found a tree covered with innumerable shreds of cloth fastened by afflicted wayfarers.

Mr. William Copeland Borlase, in his exhaustive monograph on early Christianity in Cornwall,[2] or as he names it 'The Age of the Saints,' says that 'this practice is an exact counterpart of a custom at Balmano in Scotland, and in the Orkneys, but it obtains also amongst the Yezeedes of the Persian border, the Mohammedans in Turkey, and throughout Northern Asia generally. In Japan it is still a constant usage amongst the devotees of the most ancient form of religion in that country, —the Shintooists. In the interior of the island of Niphon, I have myself witnessed pilgrims tying strips of cloth or paper to the trees as a memorial of their visit to some sacred shrine, or spring, or

[1] Quoted in Brand.

[2] *Journal of R. I. C.*, No. xx, p. 59.

waterfall; and the fact that in our own country the ceremony was performed before the sun was up, shows that in Britain it was originally what in the Orient it is still, a part and parcel of the most primitive and widely extended worship of the Sun.'

The learned Dr. O'Connor, in the third of his *Letters of Columbanus*,[1] directed against the pretensions of ultramontane Catholics, gives from his own observation much that throws light upon this matter, and derived from the only reliable source, the oral testimony of the country folk. Those letters were addressed to his brother, Owen O'Connor, Esq.

'I have often inquired of your tenants what they themselves thought of their pilgrimages to the wells of *Kill-Aracht*, *Tobbar Brighde*, *Tobbar Muir*, near Elphin, *Moor*, near *Castlereagh*, where multitudes annually assembled to celebrate what they, in broken English, termed *Patterns* (Patron's days); and when I pressed a very old man, Owen Hester, to state what possible advantage he expected to derive from the singular custom of frequenting in particular such wells as were contiguous to an old blasted oak, or an upright unhewn stone, and what the meaning was of the yet more singular custom of *sticking rags* on the branches of such trees and spitting on them, his answer, and the answer of the oldest men, was that their ancestors always did it, that it was a preservation against *Geasa Draoi-*

[1] *Columbanus's Third Letter*, etc. London: Baldwin, 1810.

decht, i.e., the sorceries of the Druids; that their cattle were preserved by it from infectious disorders; that the *daoini maithe, i.e.*, the fairies, were kept in good humour by it; and so thoroughly persuaded were they of the sanctity of these Pagan practices that they would travel bareheaded and barefooted from ten to twenty miles for the purpose of crawling on their knees round these wells, upright stones, and oak trees, westward, as the sun travels, some three times, some six, some nine, and so on in uneven numbers until their voluntary penances were completely fulfilled.'

Another writer says that 'it is impossible to pass over any considerable portion of Ireland without encountering holy wells, and rags and ribbons hung around them as memorials of the sacredness of the waters, or offerings to the tutelary saint'.[1]

At Ahagour in Mayo is a well much frequented by pilgrims, for penance chiefly, where among other offerings they cut up their clothes, be they ever so new, and tie them to the two old trees growing near, 'lest, on the day of judgment,' thinks the superstitious peasant, 'the Almighty should forget that he came there, and in order that the tokens should be known, when St. Patrick should lay them before the tribunal'.

I make these references to deduce what probably is the meaning of so ancient and extensively

[1] P. Dixon Hardy, *The Holy Wells of Ireland*, Dublin, 1836, p. 3.

existing a custom. I observe that in Ireland the resort to noted wells is yet marked by rites and observances of an older and more distinctly Pagan character than those which obtain in Cornwall; and this therefore shows that the Celtic Cornish were, not earlier certainly, but more speedily, acted on by missionary effort than our Hibernian cousins, chiefly on account of our narrower space. In Cornwall the resort to the most frequented holy well was attended by such disorderly and unseemly scenes as to require magisterial interference; and in consequence the well was shut up, and the miracle suppressed. This is now unknown among us; but in Ireland up to a late date pilgrimages, or *patterns*, as they are there called, were the occasion of such heathenish orgies that pipers, fiddlers, free libations of whisky, wild dances, fighting, quarrelling, and all manner of debaucheries, wound up a ceremony begun with penance, and ending like the festivals once held in honour of Aphrodite.

Dr. Paris, an excellent chemist, as well as a distinguished physician, tells us that analysis has been unable to detect in the water the presence of any active ingredient to explain its attributed virtues."[1]—T. Q. C.

Children used to be taken to this well on the first three Sunday mornings in May to be dipped in the water, that they might be cured of the

[1] *Guide to Mount's Bay*, by a Physician, p. 122.

rickets, or any other disorder with which they were troubled. Three times they were plunged into the water, after having been stripped naked; the parent, or person dipping them, standing facing the sun; after the dipping they were passed nine times round the well from east to west; then they were dressed and laid on St. Madern's bed; should they sleep, and the water in the well bubble, it was considered a good omen. Strict silence had to be kept during the entire performance, or the spell was broken. At the present time the people go to the well in crowds on the first Sunday in May, when the Wesleyans hold a service there, and a sermon is preached; after which the people throw in two pins or pebbles to consult the spirit, or try for sweethearts; if the two articles sink together, they will soon be married. Small crosses made of pieces of straw, fastened in the centre by a pin, are also used.

"Baptism was administered only at the stated times of Easter and Whitsuntide, but at all seasons the virtues of the waters attracted the lame and the impotent; and the altar was at hand to assist the devotion of their prayers, as well as to receive the offerings of their gratitude."[1] The custom of leaving donations was kept up until the middle of the seventeenth century, since then it has been entirely dropped.

No clue can be found as to whom St. Madron

[1] *Guide to Mount's Bay*, by a Physician.

was, or whence he came; beyond the fact that he lived in the hermitage which bears his name, nothing is known of him; there is even a diversity of opinion as to the sex of the saint, some writers speaking of him as a woman.

There is still an abundant supply of beautiful water in the well, and the villagers go there and fetch it for all household purposes, except in very wet weather, when they go to Nanceglos, the ground round St. Madron's being so marshy. The well itself is now simply a hole in the ground, with no vestige of building or stonework above or around it; but the remains of the baptistery are in much the same condition they have been for the last half-century or more.

HOLY WELL, MANATON.

Manaton farm, on which spot the old manor house once stood, is about half a mile from South-hill. In the valley below the old gardens and

MANATON WELL.

four fish ponds there is a holy well; it seems to have no saint's name attached to it, nor are there any remembered traditions or special virtues connected with its waters. The building is about five feet three inches in height, six feet eight inches in length, and four feet six inches in width; the spring over which this is erected is pure as crystal and never-failing. Large granite quoins form the walls, and the stone of the doorway is moulded; it has lately been re-roofed with turf by the present tenant of the farm, and forms a very curious and beautiful little building.

MARK'S WELL, ST. ERNEY.

The holy well at Markwell still exists; it is covered by masonry, and a copious stream runs from it which supplies water to the few inhabitants of the village. The oldest name connected with this well seems to have been Mark's Well—probably St. Mark's Well, and dedicated to the saint of that name; in later years it has been called Earl's Well, or Earl of Cornwall's Well. There are no traditions connected with it now remembered, nor is any peculiar virtue ascribed to its waters.

ST. MARTIN'S WELL, LISKEARD.

In the *History of Cornwall*, compiled by Hitchens and edited by Drew, occurs the following account of St. Martin's Well: "There is a house standing near the bottom of the town, which from its windows, gateway, and sculptured ornaments, appears to have been formerly connected with some religious establishment. Near this building issues the spring which supplies the inhabitants with water. The excellency of this salubrious fountain is deservedly held in high estimation. Conscious of its intrinsic value, the credulous inhabitants of former ages attributed to it some miraculous virtues, which fancy still continues to cherish with fondness, even to the present day. The source whence this water issues is acknowledged to be involved in a kind of indefinite mystery, so that even curiosity is content to let it remain unexplored. The stream on becoming visible is divided into three parts, all of which have some peculiar efficacy; but one branch far surpasses the others in its potent qualities. A stone that is deposited in the well is presumed by tradition to have a considerable influence over the matrimonial connections of any fortunate female, who, under given circumstances, and at an appointed time, shall have the happiness to touch it with her foot. These tales are still kept alive, and the ceremonials are practised by the young and thoughtless to the present hour."

The age became less credulous as years went by; for Gilbert in his *Survey of Cornwall*, vol. ii, writes: "Liskeard has one of the most commodious wells that we have seen in the county, and which was formerly crowded by superstitious visitors. The water falls into a stone reservoir from three shutes; and that which flows from the central one was in former times believed to possess the greatest healing efficacy. The well is still plentifully supplied with transparent water; but the credibility of its sanative virtues has evaporated like the morning dew which is exhaled by the rays of the sun."

St. Martin's Well has changed its title in these later years, and is now commonly spoken of as "Pipe Well," from the pipes through which the water flows, the number of which is now four. It stands at the back of the market-place, and is kept in a state of good repair, for its water is in general use. The magic stone is said to be still in the well, but is now covered over and its virtue gone.

ST. MARTIN'S WELL, LOOE.

This was formerly a stream (dedicated to St. Martin) flowing out of a rock; it was much used by the villagers because of the excellent quality of the water; now it is covered in with an ordinary wooden lid, and is used to supply the town of Looe with water.

ST. MAWE'S WELL, ST. JUST IN ROSELAND.

"'From St. Just pille or creks,' as Leland tells us in his minute description of Falmouth harbour, on the east, 'to St. Mauditus (Manditus) creeke, is a mile *dim.* The point of land betwixt St. Just creeke and St. Maws is of some caullid Pendinas; on this point standith as yn the entery of St. Maws creeke a castelle or forteres late begon by the king. This creke of St. Maws goeth up a two miles by est north est into the land scant a quarter of a mile from the castel; on the same side, upper into the land, is a praty village or fischar town with a pere, cawlid St. Maws; and there is a chapelle of hym, and his chaire of stone a litle without, and his welle. They caulle this sainct there St. Mat . . . ; he was a bishop in Britain, and (is) painted as a scholemaster.'[1]

"The name of this saint is so disfigured by provincial pronunciation, both in Bretagné and in Cornwall, that we should hardly recognise Maclovius in Machutus and Machu, if all the names were not used by the *same* biographer for the *same* person,[2] and should never believe St. Maudite, St.

[1] Leland's *Itin.*, iii, 29, 30. [2] Leland's *Col.*, ii, 430, 432.

Mat, or St. Mawe of the island, to be the very Machu, Machutus, or Maclovius of the continent, if the former had not been averred to have been, what we know the latter was, a bishop in Bretagné.

St. Mawe's Well.

This stroke of traditional history rivets all the links of intelligence into one chain. With this around us we recognise, we revere, the saint of Wales, and the prelate of Bretagné, as once a resident upon the shores of Cornwall, and at the side of Falmouth harbour. The well, the chair, and the chapel, like those of another saint upon another part of our coast, as I shall speedily show, combine to mark the residence of the saint at the place. He came to Corsult in the 'Daumonian region,' in that half of it which is now called Cornwall, and in that part of it, his half, which was then denominated Corsult, but is now the parish of St. Just.[1]

"In his way *from* Wales undoubtedly, when he had leisure for such a work, and *not* (as his biographer says) on some occasional return *to* Wales, *when* he was too fully employed for such a business, he settled at a point of the seashore here, then all solitary in itself, and merely a long sloping descent of rock to the water, with a broad leafy heath at the back of it, I believe, giving appellation to the whole.

. . . .

"The existence of a well combined with the solitariness of the site and with the warmth of the rocky bank facing the noon-day sun to invite his settlement at this particular ground. There he lived as a hermit; forming himself a chair in the rock above the well for his enjoyment of the warm situation, in occasional surveys of the creek under him, of the harbour upon his right, and of the sea in front of the latter, then all assuredly solitary almost as his very site itself.

[1] So we have Carsella in St. Dennis, and Corsullan in St. Keverne.

"Thence, however, the fame of his sanctity diffused itself over the neighbourhood, as we have previously seen it do in the vicinity of St. Maloe's, the world of Christians *then* turning with attention and reverence to every character particularly religious, considering themselves only as citizens of earth for a few years. . . .

"He thus became troubled probably with the resort of people to him, removed across the Channel to find a more solitary situation, and settled in an uninhabited islet for the effectual preclusion of all visits. The shortness of the passage into France, and the known predominance of Christianity equally in Cornwall as in Wales, had, in all probability, brought him hither at first; and he *now* took the short passage which he had formerly intended to take; crossing over directly to the opposite shore of St. Maloe's. . . . After his removal, the chair and the well appear to have been visited and admired for his sake, the admiration of his character naturally attaching to every object connected with it, and the body being honoured from respect to the soul that lately inhabited it. After he was dead and sainted, this admiration of course rose into reverence, the well was visited in greater crowds, the chair was viewed with deeper respect, and the hermitage was entered with devouter awe.

"This gave a commencement to the town, the votaries of the sainted hermit settling in houses around his hermitage, and the hermitage itself being reconstructed into a chapel for their devotions. This continued all to the Reformation, the reverence having its foundation in religion, and the devoutness raising its head towards heaven; when, amidst the many blessings attendant upon that revolution in the Church, one evil prevailed in slighting the characters of the saints; in withdrawing the honours paid to their names, even in dilapidating or desecrating the fanes dedicated to their memories. *At* the Reformation the well was still attended, with a respect that was called, and perhaps has mounted into, superstition; the chair still remained all of solid stone in the cemetery of the chapel, reported even then by tradition to have been *frequently* used by the saint; and the chapel itself still exhibited a portrait of its patron, 'painted as a scholemaster,' in the loose gown, I believe, still worn frequently by schoolmasters in the north of England, yet equally worn by clergymen of the north or south in their studies at present.

"But now—when the 'praty village or fischar town with a pere' has been exalted into a parliamentary borough—all is gone. . . . Only the well appears cut deeply in the living rock, on the right of the road into the village; running endlong into the heart of the rock, arched over for its whole length, and faced with a slightly peaked arch of stone. The water is good, but rather hard; and the fountain is still denominated pre-eminently above others that are in the village, St. Mawe's Well.

"Close to it on the south, but lower on the descent of the hill, was the chapel, well known by tradition to have been such, and reported by that tradition to have *fallen into ruins*; before the aged-seeming stones were worked up again into the present dwelling-house. . . . Over the well, along the northern side of the chapel, and two or three yards above the level of it, was the chapel-yard; still remaining in an open area above the well itself, but built upon for the remainder. The buildings, however, were raised within memory, and human bones were dug up in laying the foundations. . . . Thus, in strict propriety, the well is all that we see at present of St. Mawe's memorials here."[1]

At the present time it is a favourite resort of picnic parties, pins are dropped in, and wishes made, as is the case with so many of the holy wells. This is probably an innovation of later years, arising from the desire of the visitors to find pleasure and amusement.

[1] Whitaker's *Cathedral of Cornwall.*

St. Melor's Well, Linkinghorne, 1891.

ST. MELOR'S WELL, LINKINGHORNE.

At the bottom of a field not far from the church this pretty well is situated; but not until one is close upon it can one see it, the field being very steep, and the well standing in a level three-cornered piece of ground close under the brow of the hill.

The little structure is composed of large blocks of granite, and is perfect as far as the building is concerned, save for the chipping off a corner of the block which forms the backbone of the roof, and at the same time the arch of a large niche over the broadly arched entrance. There are two more niches within the building, one on the left-hand side of the doorway, and the other, a square one, at the back. In one of the side pillars are iron staples, which lead one to suppose there was at one time a door, but it has now disappeared.

A clear and copious stream flows from the well, making the ground around a perfect marsh, where rushes and other water plants flourish abundantly. But no tradition hangs round this well, nor is any virtue attributed to its water. St. Melor, to whom it is dedicated, does not seem to have ever visited the spot; and, in all probability, the well received its name when the church was dedicated to that saint.

"Melor," says an ancient history of his life, as extracted by Leland, "was the son of Melian, *king* of Cornwall; Haurilla, the daughter of Earl Rivold, and born in Devonshire, was the mother of St. Melor; Rivold, 'the son of the other Rivold, and brother of Haurilla,' became the murderer of his brother 'Melian,' and the invader of Cornwall; *he deprived his nephew Melor of one foot and one hand;* Melor was bred up in a monastery . . . Melor, *at the suggestion of his uncle* Rivold, was murdered by his own foster-father Cerealtine."[1]

"Melor therefore was the son, not of a duke of Cornwall, as no duke existed there for ages after Melor, but of a *king*. Nor did he, as Dr. Borlase and his authors agree to intimate, ever suffer martyrdom for Christianity. He died under the hand of that ambition which is so wildly fermenting in the heart of man at times, and now acted the demon so savagely in this king of Devonshire. Melor's maternal uncle invaded the country of Cornwall, seized the person of Melor's father, the king, and murdered him; but was content for the present with only maiming Melor himself by cutting off one hand and one foot; yet afterwards instigated the very man who by the customs of Britain was next to Melor's own father in relationship to him, even his foster-father, to murder him. Such a complication of villainies, meeting in the murder of Melor, the son of a king,

1 Leland's *Itin.*, 394.

a king himself by the murder of his father and a Christian as bred up in a monastery, induced the Christians of Cornwall, his and his father's subjects, to consider him a martyr in their minds, and to rank him as a martyr in their calendars."[1]

[1] Whitaker's *Cathedral of Cornwall.*

MENACUDDLE WELL.

"This very pretty and carefully preserved well is on the ornamental grounds of Mr. Martin, near St. Austell town, and it is pleasant to see what tender care he takes of it. It stands, enveloped in foliage, in a vale at the foot of Menacuddle grove, surrounded by romantic scenery. Its length, without, is eleven feet, its breadth nine feet; height of the gable end eleven feet. The doorways, five feet two inches high, and two feet nine inches in breadth, are opposite each other, facing due north and south. The large granite stones which compose them are neatly moulded; the shafts ending in ornamental capitals, from which, in each case, springs an equilateral arch. There is a small window in the western side, while the eastern is embedded in the hill from which the water issues. This water is caught as it flows in a granite basin, divided by a partition stone, and flows from one division into the other. It is very pure and good, and, in the estimation of the country people, possessed of extraordinary virtues for cure, and also prophecy. 'Weakly children were carried thither to be bathed,' according to Samuel Drew, a native of St. Austell; 'ulcers have also been washed in its sacred water, and people, in seasons of sickness, have been recommended by the neighbouring matrons to drink of the salubrious fluid. In most of these cases instances may be procured of benefits received from the application, but the prevailing opinion is that the advantages enjoyed result rather from some mystical virtue attributed to the water for ages past, than from its natural qualities. Within the memory of persons now living, this well was a place of general resort for the young and thoughtless. On approaching the margin, each visitor, if he hoped for good luck through life, was expected to throw a crooked pin into the water; and it was presumed that the other pins, which had been deposited there by former devotees, might be seen rising from their beds to meet it before it reached the bottom. But though many have gazed with eager expectation, no one has yet been permitted to witness the traditionary phenomenon.'[1]

At Menacuddle, and in the near neighbourhood of the well, was once a free chapel, subject to the Priory of Tywardreath. Dr. Oliver, in his abridgment of the certificates of chantries and colleges for Devon and Cornwall, mentions a free chapel of Benecuddle, and thinks it must be that of which we speak. It was founded by the ancestors of Peryse (qu. Penrice, an estate now and for many years the seat of Sir Charles Sawle, Baronet, formerly of the family of Penrice), to find a priest to celebrate certain masses 'in the parish church

[1] *History of Cornwall*, vol. i, p. 534.

of Benecuddle, and he to be deacon unto the vicar there at festival times in celebration of the mass'.

MENACUDDLE WELL.

The yearly value of the lands and possession was said to be vi*li*.

The chantry within the church of *Menacuttell* is mentioned in Bishop Vesey's Register, vol. i, fol. vii."—T. Q. C.

The well is in much the same state now as it was when the accompanying sketch was made. On making personal inquiries about it there seemed to be some confusion as to its name, some speaking of it as "Menacuddle Well," and others as "Trethowel Well," until one almost began to think there must be two wells: the fact is that Menacuddle estate is on one hill and Trethowel on the opposite, the well being in the valley between, but on the Trethowel side of the road; Menacuddle, however, seems to have been its oldest name. It is a beautiful little Gothic building, and is still used as a wishing-well, if one may judge from the pins which lie in its granite basin. Mr. Martin, mentioned above, no longer lives at Menacuddle.

ST. MEWAN'S WELL.

The Rev. W. S. Lach-Szyrma, writing on the subject of the early history of the Church in Cornwall, mentions that "St. Mewan seems to have been a popular saint in Cornwall, and has given name to three parishes—Mewan, Mythian, and also, with St. Issy, to Mevagissey. . . . St. Mewan was a Welsh man, of Gwent, a cousin of St. Sampson, who founded in Brittany a famous monastery of St. Meen."

In spite of this above-mentioned popularity very little indeed is known of St. Mewan; he is seldom mentioned, and the people of St. Mewan know of no legend or tradition connected with their parish; in fact, they have never heard of the saint except as a name for their parish. Of the well nothing can be said except that the stream still runs along at the bottom of a field on the vicarage glebe. There is neither history nor legend attached to it; no interest is taken in it, no building stands over it, nor are there any stones lying near which might suggest that it had been enclosed in times past; and the only mention found referring to this spring is in the *Parochial History of Cornwall*, where the following paragraph occurs: "In a field adjoining the rectory is a dilapidated well, supposed to have been anciently a baptistery; its restoration is intended".

HOLY WELL, MICHAELSTOW

Is prettily situated in the churchyard opposite the south door. It is in fair preservation, at least what remains of it seems firm and well cared for, but it was evidently rather an elaborate structure at one time. There is a short inclined way down to it, and stones on either side lead one to think there was at one time a covered building of some importance.

Wallis, in his *Parochial History of Cornwall*, says: "There are also the ruins of an ancient baptistery, the restoration of which is intended". At present it is, like so many others, just an ordinary walled well in a hollow of the sloping churchyard; there is no building over it, only a square stone front, grown over with grass and delicate ferns; beautiful hart's-tongues line the interior, and large trees overshadow the whole.

The water, which is still used for baptisms, is little more than half a foot in depth, but except in an exceptionally severe drought there is a constant supply.

The parish church is dedicated to St. Michael.

WELL OF ST. MORWENNA.

The saint who gives her name to this well was the daughter, or at least one of the family, of Brechan, or Brychan, a king of Wales; Brechan is reputed to have had a very large family, the number varying, according to different accounts, from twenty-four to forty-nine; in the longer list it is probable that his grandchildren were included, which would account for the decided discrepancy. Morwenna is said to have migrated from Wales to Cornwall, and established herself at Morwenstow—the parish taking its name from her—erecting her cell on the cliff overlooking the Atlantic, from whence, on a clear day, she could see the hills of her native country. It has often been erroneously said that Morwenna was an Irish woman, but this arose probably from a very natural confusion of her name with that of Modwenna.

The Rev. S. Baring-Gould, in his book *The Vicar of Morwenstow*, writes of the well as follows: "Half-way down Morwenstow cliff, only to be reached by a narrow and scarcely distinguishable path, is the well of St. Morwenna. Mr. Hawker repaired it; but about twenty years ago the spring worked itself away through another stratum of slate, and sprung out of the sheer cliff some feet lower down, and falls in a miniature cascade, a silver thread of water, over a ledge of schist into the sea. On a green spot across which now run cart tracks, in the side of the glen, stood originally, according to Mr. Hawker, a chapel to St. Morwenna, visited by those who sought her sacred well. The green patch forms a rough parallelogram, and bears faint traces of having been levelled out of the slope. No stone remains on another of this ancient chapel." Mr. Baring-Gould also gives the legend that when Morwenna lay dying her brother Nectan came to her from Hartland, and she requested him to raise her in his arms that her eyes might last rest on her native Wales. "And so she died on Morwenstow cliff, looking out across the Severn sea to the faint blue line of the Welsh mountains."

The cliff on which St. Morwenna's well is situated is known as the "Vicarage Cliff"; the well itself is in a patch of thorns; over the spot is a squarely shaped building with a cross on the roof, but the spring is dry at present.

NANCEGLOS, NEAR PENZANCE.

A large stone well, said to be a wishing-well, but of no repute now save for the excellence of its water.

There was also a wishing-well in the Bone Valley; it is now only a small stream, and is not used for purposes of divination.

HOLY WELL OF OUR LADY OF NANTS, COLAN.

" Dear old Carew—to whom we owe so much of what our forefathers were like; tillers, tinners, rich and poor, their civil government and even their recreations--tells us this respecting Lady Nant's Well of his day; for he did not, in his attention to the past, neglect to make record of the present :—

'Little Colan hath lesse worth the observation, unlesse you will deride or pity their simplicity who sought at our Lady Nant's Well there to foreknowe what fortune should betide them, which was in this maner :—

'Upon Palm Sunday, these idle-headed seekers resorted thither with a palme crosse in one hand, and an offring in the other; the offring fell to the priest's share, the crosse they threw into the well; which if it swamme the party should outlive that yeere; if it sunk, a short ensuing death was boded, and not perhaps altogether untruely, while a foolish conceyt of this halsening might sooner helpe it onwards. A contrary practise to the goddess *Junoes* lake in Laconia: for there if the wheaten cakes cast in upon her festivall day were by the water receiued, it betokened good luck; if rejected, euill. The like is written by *Pausanias* of Inus in Greece, and by others touching the offrings throwne into the fornace of Mount Etna in Sicily.'

Norden, following Carew a few years after, gives a similar account of the well, which would seem to have been the most notable thing in the parish.

There is, I believe, no subsequent mention of Lady Nant's Well by Cornish historians. At present the old spring runs on and is likely to run on for ever, giving the villagers healthful water for all natural purposes, its supernatural qualities unknown and uninvoked. Except to a few who have heard of its extraordinary endowments from books, it is simply a stream of excellent water. The clergyman tells me there is no architectural building about it; nothing to mark its old sanctity.[1] An old woman told him that when she was a girl no other water than that of the well (though situate at some distance from the church) was ever used for baptism. This seems to have been the last lingering trace of the old reverence for the Holy Well of our Lady."—T. Q. C.

1 The Rev. Arthur Adams, vicar, ann. 1883.

ST. NEOT'S WELL.

"In a pleasant valley, deeply set in an amphitheatre of high hill and higher table-land of moor and tor, threaded by a brook wending its way to the river Fowey, the saintly anchoret Neot settled down, somewhere about the middle of the ninth century. He was of noble, some say of kingly, birth. Learned, pious, and austere of habit, in his wooded cell he was visited from far and near for advice and help in matters spiritual and bodily. Even King Alfred the Great, a near relative (it is said his brother), came hither to consult him. This is traditional, and not strictly vouched for. The stories which even Asser, his biographer, has told us, have in these times been doubted. The king hiding for safety, the cowherd's wife, and the burnt cake, have been made questions of historic doubt. It is, however, a plain fact that St. Neot in this sequestered dell is still surrounded by a halo of legend, and that the well, the crow's pound, the storied windows richly dight, and heaps of country-side stories, still attest that this great little man (for he was of dwarfish stature) is not altogether fabulous. In the unique church dedicated to him, the windows tell his story. Here he resigns his crown to his younger brother, after having taken his vows as a monk. He is sitting chanting his psalter, his daily wont, his feet in the sacred well. Here a hunted fawn flying from

St. Neot's Well.

its pursuers seeks the well, and falling before the holy man mutely and pantingly beseeches his protection. The dogs are abashed and fly. The huntsman, throwing away his quiver, delivers up his horn to the saint, and immediately becomes a monk.

The well, which, as far as I can find, never had any architectural interest, became much ruined by age, and was restored by the Rev. Henry Grylls, the vicar. Mitchell, in his *Parochial History of St. Neot*, said of it some fifty years ago, that 'near this well, which is about half a mile west of the church, Neot resided as a hermit with his attendant Barius, and communicated that reputed holiness which still adheres in part to its waters. That there was an arch of stone over it, with a large oak springing from the arch, and with doors to the entrance, was remembered by some old inhabitants of the parish lately deceased. This beautiful spring, with a rill issuing from it, that constantly supplies the neighbouring village with the purest water, is yet to be seen at the foot of a steep hill. About seventy years since, the very large and spreading oak which grew horizontally from the bank above and overshadowed the well in a fan-like form was cut down by the tenant of the estate for repairs, when it had been spared for centuries, probably from a principle of religion. Weakly children used within memory to be brought here.'

One of the designs in the church windows tells the story of the well. Neot receives instructions from an angel respecting three fishes which he shows him in this fountain. The directions were, that so long as he took one, and only one, of the fishes for his daily food, the supply should never be diminished. The saint, sick in bed, orders his servant to bring one of the fish for his dinner. Barius, anxious to gratify his master, incautiously takes two of the fishes, boils one and roasts the other, probably to meet his taste. Poor Barius, over-troubled about much serving his sick master, brings the fish to the bedside; whereupon the saint, alarmed at this breach of the angel's injunctions, orders Barius to take the two cooked fishes to the well and throw them in. The fishes are immediately restored to life."—T. Q. C.

This well of St. Neot is now covered by a substantial building, the roof is formed of three blocks of solid granite, the broad arched doorway is also of granite, as are the side blocks and the three steps which lead down to the water. It has a wooden door studded with iron nails, and a cross rises from the roof. From the bank above grows an oak, and although it has not the "fan-like form" of that which once overshadowed the well, it is a very fine tree. The water runs into the well at one corner; it is not now used as a cure for weakly children, but is generally considered very good.

ST. NUN'S WELL, ALTARNON.

"Carew gives, I believe, the first, and certainly the fullest, account of this well.

"'In our forefathers' days, when devotion as much exceeded knowledge as knowledge now cometh short of devotion, there were many *bowssening* places for curing madmen; and amongst the rest, one at Alternunne in this hundred, called St. Nunne's Pool, which saint's altar it may be, *pars pro toto*, gave name to the church. And because the maner of this bowssening is not so unpleasing to heare as it was uneasie to feele, I wil (if you please) deliver you the practise as I receyved it from the beholder.

'The water running from St. Nunne's Well fell into a square and close-walled plot, which might bee filled at what depth they listed. Upon this wall was the franticke person set to stand, his backe towards the poole; and from thence, with a sudden blow in the brest, tumbled headlong into the pond, where a strong fellowe, provided for the nonce, tooke him and tossed him and tossed him, up and downe, alongst and athwart the water, until the patient, by forgoing his strength, had somewhat forgot his fury. Then was hee conveyed to the church, and certaine masses sung over him;

upon which handling, if his right wits returned, St. Nunne had the thanks; but, if there appeared small amendment, he was bowssened againe, and againe, while there remayned in him any hope of life for recovery.

'It may be, this device tooke original from that master of Bedlem, who (the fable saith) used to cure his patients of that impatience, by keeping them bound in pooles up to the middle, and so more or less after fit of their fury.' "[1]—T. Q. C.

St. Nun (see St. Nun's Well, Pelynt, p. 175) was the mother of St. David of Wales. Of this saint the Rev. W. S. Lach-Szyrma writes as follows: "His mother [St. David's], St. Nonna, is remembered at St. Nunn's Well, and at Altarnun, the altar of St. Nonn (where probably she was buried). It is said she was no nun, but a famous beauty of the period—a Cornish girl, and daughter of a Cornish chief—with whom King Cereticus (a later corruption of Caractacus) fell in love, and whom he married, and who bore him a son, the famous Bishop St. David. William of Worcester even states that St. David was born at Altarnun in Cornwall, and thus was by birth a Cornishman." It is interesting to note that as St. Non's Well is near St. David's Cathedral in Wales, so here Davidstowe adjoins the parish of Altarnon.

[1] *Survey of Cornwall*, ed. 1769, p. 122. Carew mentions that the administrator of this heroic treatment was Schimpfund Ernst.

Drew, in his *History of Cornwall*, writes: "Alluding to the opinion of Mr. Carew, Mr. Hals observes that 'the word Altar in this place is not to be construed as a derivative from Altare, an altar on which offerings or sacrifices were made by fire, or otherwise, at this pool. But rather the chancel of the present church was a chapel pertaining to the nuns or nunnery once here, afterwards augmented and converted to a parish church, as it now stands, and that the ground whereon the vicarage house is now extant was of old the nunnery house itself, wherein those virgins resided; the stones and materials of which old house are concerted in the new vicarage, brave mansion. And to prove this tradition, there yet appears in the fields the channel, or water-course, by which the waters of St. Nun's Pool were carried into this old nunnery house in former ages.' From these circumstances he concludes that the name Altar Nun should be interpreted as a corruption of, or deviation from, *Alter Nun*, to alter or change from one thing to another; namely, from that of a nunnery of religious votaresses, to that of a parochial and church vicarage, from whence it has its denomination." But Gilbert, in his *History of Cornwall*, writes: "The site of the parsonage was formerly occupied by a religious house, dedicated to St. Nun, whence originated the name of the church and parish. The altar of St. Nun was long held in peculiar veneration by the country people. Among the early interments in this church, or rather, we may suppose, a former one, which occupied the same ground, was that of St. Nonnet, or St. Nun, mother of St. David, who, according to her legend (quoted by William of Worcester), was born here." This derivation of the name *Altarnon* seems to be the one generally accepted. The 2nd March is dedicated to St. Nun, and said formerly to have been observed in Wales.

The well is situated at the bottom of a field near the Vicarage, and the present vicar of the parish, Rev. A. H. Malan, has done his best to preserve what remains of it; a fence has been erected on one side, which, with two hedges, forms a triangular plot enclosing the spring, and protecting it from cattle, which are probably answerable for the entire destruction of the walls—those same walls which, according to Carew, must have formed a kind of Roman bath. The well itself is sadly overgrown with rank grass and weeds, and the spring is now entirely dry, owing to the draining of the field adjoining; its three walls—back, and two sides—which have been repaired, are the old work, in fact this is all that is really left of St. Nun's Well. A covering stone has been placed over the top; an old thorn grows close by, and some carved stones lie in the well at present, but these are not belonging to any of the old building, they having been brought from the adjacent sanctuary meadow and placed there.

ST. NUN'S WELL, PELYNT.

"On the western side of the beautiful cleft through which the Trelawne river flows to join the Looe estuary, and near Hobb's Park, in the parish of Pelynt, is St. Nun's, or, according to the country folk, St. Ninnie's Well. It is sometimes called the Piskie's Well. Its position when I first knew it was only to be found by an old oak tree clothed with ivy and a dense undergrowth of willow and bramble which grew unrestrainedly above and around.

This well had been protected from the violating hand of man by a story which had been told of it for ages. Time, and the storms of winter, however, had been slowly ruining it. The oak which grew upon its roof had, by its roots, dislodged several stones of the arch, and swaying about in the wind had shaken down a large mass of masonry. I communicated the ruinous condition of the well to the Trelawnys of Trelawne, the owners of it; and, at their request, I had the pleasure of superintending the restoration of the well. For this it was necessary to fell the tree, and make a general clearance, which disclosed a building of which the following is a description.

The front of the well is upright to about four

feet, from which starts a pointed front. A rude entrance, about four feet high, is spanned above by a single flat stone as lintel, and leads to a

St. Ninnie's Well, Pelynt.

dim grotto with an arched roof. Above the door is a square recess, without ornament.[1] The inside

[1] "In my temporary absence the silly mason, notwithstanding my instructions, had made this triangular, as it will now be found to be, and as it figured in Blight's engraving, p. 79."

of the well is draped with the luxuriant fronds of hart's-tongue and black spleenwort ferns, on a rich bed of moss and liverwort. At the farther end of the floor is a round granite basin with a deeply moulded brim, ornamented lower and all round its circumference with a series of rings, each enclosing a Greek cross or ball. The water must be supplied from an opening at the back; for none runs into it from the rim, and yet it is always full. If emptied, it soon fills again. Though near a public road it is entirely concealed from public view—dropped as it is on the side of a steep hill—and is only reached by a flight of steps.

This interesting antiquity has, as I have said, been guarded by a legendary tale which I have here put upon written record, and can only wish that some such traditions had been attached to our cromlechs, circles, maenhirs, way-side crosses, wells, *et quibusdam aliis*, which have been ruined under our eyes, or are in process of ruination.

An old farmer once set his eyes upon the granite basin, and coveted it; for it was not wrong in his regard to convert the holy font to the base uses of the pigsty. One day he drove his oxen and wain to the gateway above, with intent to remove it. Taking his beasts to the entrance of the well, and fixing his chains around the sculptured trough, he tried to drag it from its ancient bed. For a long time it resisted the tugs of the oxen, but at length they started it and pulled it laboriously up-hill to where the wain was standing.

When nearly up it burst away from the chains, rolled down towards the well, and, making a sharp turn, rolled into its own old place. No one will again venture to displace it, seeing that . . . a man thriving and well-to-do in the world never prospered from that day forward. Indeed, retribution overtook him on the spot, the oxen falling dead, and their owner being struck lame and speechless. No one since has been hardy enough to try the removal of the font.

The well, and a small chapel above it, the remains of which are some indistinct mounds, and a vallum, artificially made, on the north and south sides (occasionally the plough turns some shaped stones and roofing slates), were dedicated to St. Nonnet, or St. Nun, a holy woman said to be the mother of St. David, and the daughter of a Cornish chief. She is also said to have lived and died at Altarnun.

In the list of parish churches and chapels, and the saints to whom they are dedicated, given in Oliver's *Monasticon Exoniense*, the name is written S. Nynninæ; in the *Inquisitiones Nonarum* (A.D. 1342) it is S. Neomena; whilst the oratory is mentioned in the Rate of Pope Nicholas IV as Capella Sce. Niemyne, and is set down elsewhere as being licensed by Bishop Stafford in the year 1400. There is another church and well dedicated to this saint at Altarnun, of which more in its proper place.

The people of the neighbourhood know the

spring by the names St. Ninnie's, St. Nun's, and Pisky's Well. I think that the latter, after all, is the oldest name, and that it was anciently believed to be the haunt of some beneficent elf, who here dispensed her bounties in the shape of health and good fortune when her fountain was reverently consulted, but could show enduring anger to those who desecrated it. The guardianship in later and much altered times was usurped by the saint whose name it usually bears. This belief in elfish tutelage of wells is common among the Celtic people. Dr. O'Connor[1] tells us that in some parts of Ireland there is a belief that by some of their ceremonies at the "patterns," or pilgrimages to wells, the *daoini maethe* (*i.e.*, fairies) were propitiated. In the basin of St. Nun's may be found a great number of pins, thrown in by those who avail themselves of the curative qualities of its water, or consult it for intimations of the future. I was curious to know what meaning the unlettered peasantry attached to this strange but common custom; and on asking an old man at work near, was told that it was done 'to get the good-will of the piskies,' who after the tribute of a pin ceased to mislead them, gave them good health, and made fortunate the operations of husbandry."—T. Q. C.

This well when visited in July, 1891, was in a very fair state of preservation, though not now

[1] *Letters of Columbanus*, iii.

used for any particular purpose. A thorn and a nut tree overshadow it, and ivy creeps from between the masonry. Ferns and mosses grow luxuriantly in the interior, where the trough still stands, into which were cast pins in former days; but the surrounding ground was in such a marshy state as to make it impossible to approach near enough to examine any carving which may be on it. A woman, on directing us to the spot, smilingly spoke of having visited the well for the purpose of divination in her younger days; an old man, who stood by, remarked that no one he had ever heard of knew when or why the well was built there,—but that was very possible,—he had heard that people had attempted to move it, with no success.

HOLY WELL, PELYNT.

On the grounds of Hall Park, close to the village of Pelynt, is another holy well. No building now marks it, nor has been known to exist within the last thirty years, at any rate. The inmates of the farm declared the spot to be quite inaccessible at the time of our visit, owing to the late rains. There are no stones remaining to show that this well had at any time a building or covering over it; it is simply an open spring which still goes by the name of " Holy Well," and the water, though considered particularly good, has no especial virtues attributed to it.

PENVENTON WELL, LEWANNICK.

This well, which is situated at the extreme south quarter of the parish, is, except to the vicar, almost entirely unknown now. It is simply an open stream, overgrown with brambles and weeds; with no masonry over it, and no sign that there has ever been any.

One of the oldest inhabitants of the parish has stated that in olden times the water for baptisms was brought from this well, but the custom has long since been discontinued, which is not to be wondered at, considering the well is at least two miles from the village, and that there are so many good streams within easy distance of the church.

The village of Lewannick is extremely well supplied with water, two springs being especially worthy of notice, although they have no claims to holiness.

Blaunders Well, the existence of which is by some considered the origin of the foundation of the village, is a most remarkable one,—its flow of water is simply inexhaustible even in the driest season, when all parishioners and cattle get their supply from it.

On the Trelaske estate is a well named *Joan's*

Pitcher, the water of which is considered good for sore eyes.

. . . .

On the road from Lewannick to Launceston at a place called Holy Way Cross—where the turnpike gate formerly stood—is a small deep well, at the foot of the hedge, by the side of the road; by some believed to be a holy well. The water is clear and pure, a profusion of ferns grows at the back. The opening of the well is about two feet each way, rough flat stones form the sides, and one large slab of stone the top. There is nothing to distinguish it from any other wayside well; but the fact of its being so near the cross gives credence to the idea that it was used by pilgrims.

ST. PIRAN'S WELL.

St. Piran, who is accounted the patron saint of tinners, was an Irishman by birth, and a disciple of St. Patrick; he was born "in the region of Ossery, and bred up in the islet that gives denomination to Cape Clear". Becoming converted he went to Rome, was there baptised, ordained, and raised to high rank. About the year 402 he returned to Ireland, after an absence of twenty years; and converted his mother Wingela, and many of his countrymen. Desiring a hermit's solitary life, he retired to a small hermitage, at a place called after him "Sier Keran," in Leinster; but this cell grew to such an extent, his fame spreading, and the reverence felt for him inducing so many to come and settle near him, that he left and came to Cornwall, where he settled in an isolated spot in the north-east. "S. Piranes in the sandes is an xviii miles from St. Ies upward on the Severne," says Leland. "Here is a chapel erected on the sands to *St. Piran*, a saint *even of Ireland, who rests at this place*," adds Camden.

There was a tradition amongst the tinners and miners, who formed the principal population of that part of Cornwall, that St. Piran gave them some advice, and told them a valuable secret concerning the dressing and preparing of tin. This story meets with little belief now, but the fact remains that the saint was held in great veneration and esteem by the people. "These parishioners of St. Piran," says Whitaker, "have given the tone to all the tinners of the county, and exalted St. Piran into the patronage of them all. They all keep his feast upon the 5th March, hold a fair near his church upon the same day, and have near the road to Mitchell from the west, at a distance of two or three miles from the church, an arched fountain, denominated Fenton Berran lately, but Piran Well now, the very well undoubtedly by which he fixed his hermitage, and from which he drew his beverage." The water possessed healing virtues, being especially valuable in curing rickets.

About thirty years ago, the building over the well was being destroyed by the Goths of the district; when Mr. Peters, a gentleman residing at Chiverton, near Truro, heard of it; he rescued a part and had it brought and erected on his estate, where it now stands. In its original condition it had an entrance porch large enough for three or four people to sit down in, but only the broad arch of that portion was rescued; it is now placed over the arch of the well-door.

"But so brightly did the reputation of St. Piran break out from the darkness of his hermitage at Fenton Berran, and in such a broad flash of lustre did it lighten over all Cornwall, that a parish far removed to the south-west has been long dedicated to him, and is called Piran Uthno, or Little Piran, at this day; that another parish to the south-west, though not so remote, equally adopted his name many ages ago, as I shall instantly show; and that a chapelry in the parish of Stythians is now called Piran Arworthal, or Piran Well, the latter name being derived from 'a strong chalybeate spring, much frequented of late years'."—*Tonkin.*

WELL AT POLRUAN.

On the hill which slopes up from the quay at Polruan is an old moor-stone cross, which appears to have been mounted on a base of new stone; it stands on a raised bank, and underneath gushes out a never-failing stream of water from a stone mouth into a granite trough. There seems to be no legend connected with this spring; but from its propinquity to the ruins of St. Saviour's chapel on the cliff, which was formerly connected with a monastery of some importance, it is possible that its waters may have been consecrated; the cross surmounting the spring seems rather to favour the idea.

ST. PRATT'S, OR ST. PROTUS'S WELL, BLISLAND.

Of the saint who gave his name to this well we can find but little information; there seems to be no remembered legend either connected with him or his well. Maclean writes of St. Pratt in the following words: "St. Protus, together with St. Hyacinthus, were commemorated by the Church on 11th September. They were among the most illustrious martyrs who sealed their faith with their blood when the emperors of the world attempted, with all their power, to crush the little flock of Christ. It appears from the works of Pope Damascus that they were brothers. In the Acts of St. Eugenia their martyrdom is placed in the Valerian persecution in 257; but the Liberian calendar, drawn up in the pontificate of Liberius, shows that they suffered under Diocletian in 304, and that their festival was celebrated at their tomb on the Old Salarian Way on 11th September."

About fifty years ago St. Pratt's Well consisted of a shallow unwalled stream under a high bank on which a thorn bush grew; but a certain Mr. John Tom, a local Wesleyan preacher, when in the office of waywarden, tore down the bank and covered the well, the water from which now flows in a never-failing stream, some fifty-four feet below, from what is termed a "shute". Formerly the sexton fetched all water used for baptisms from St. Pratt's Well; and the late rector affirmed that in his younger days he had heard it said, and very probably it was believed, that the water used in building the church was brought from this well. At one time a fine cross of Greek form is said to have stood over the well, but it was thrown down about 1840 and sunk into the ground close by.

Some time ago Sir Warwick Morshead spoke of restoring St. Pratt's Well, but he has now given up all idea of so doing.

PROBUS HOLY WELL.

The water of this well still remains, but the only structure over it is a pump of most modern manufacture. The man of whom we made inquiries told us that it was always a shallow well, but never dry. The water is considered good; and our informant remarked that he had guided numbers of visitors to the spot, and many had made a point of drinking the water. But we could hear of no traditions. From its nearness to the church and its undoubtedly sacred nature, it was very probably the well of SS. Probus and Grace, the patron saints of the church.

WELL AT RIALTON PRIORY.

This well stands in the courtyard adjoining Rialton Priory; it has no legend or tradition connected with it, but from its very situation seems likely to have been a consecrated spring. Lysons, in his *Magna Britannica*, describes it as having "a small stone building over it, at one end of which is a niche with a pedestal for an image". Many years ago, about 1840, this building was carried off to Somersetshire by the order of the steward of the period, and was set up in private grounds there; but by order of its owners (it belongs to the Crown) it was brought back again and re-erected on its rightful spot, the steward being dismissed. The present occupier of Rialton Mills, who has kindly responded to inquiries about the well, says that this happened not a great many years ago; he knew the persons who carted the stone, and they have not been dead more than ten years. The building is now in a very good state of preservation, and much resorted to by artists for sketching purposes, and by a great number of the visitors during the summer. The water is excellent, and never-failing even in the hottest season,—*viz.*, the much-quoted "jubilee" year. It is in general use for drinking and domestic purposes.

TRELOY WELL, NEAR RIALTON.

At the top of Treskeys hill, in an orchard known as Treloy orchard, is a fairly celebrated holy well, in good preservation and much resorted to by artists and other visitors. No one appears to remember that it ever possessed any saintly name, or that there were any particular legends or ancient ceremonies connected with it. Some suggest that in addition to supplying water to the Arundells, whose property it was, it also supplied it to the monks at Rialton; but this seems rather improbable, considering the monks possessed a well close at hand in their own courtyard at the priory. The water is considered particularly good and never-failing; the building over it is of fair size with stone seats. Although nothing is remembered of its holy origin, its sanctity has always been a thing taken for granted; and the fact that a chapel once stood near it seems sufficient to dismiss all doubt on the subject.

Holy Well, Roche.

ROCHE HOLY WELL.

"Not far from the road from Bodmin to Truro over the Goss-moors, and at the head of a little hollow through which runs a tributary brooklet to the Camel, is this interesting little well. The traveller seeking it will, a short way west of Victoria, find a roadway to the right, leading down a narrow lane to some cottages. The cottagers who take their water from the spring will direct him to it, and tell him of its mystic qualities.

This well, which I once figured for Mr. Blight, and which appears in his *Crosses, etc., of East Cornwall*, must have been at one time a fairly ornate one. It is much ruined now; but the fabric having been massively built of large blocks of granite originally, and the well still ministering to the daily needs, and occasionally helping the sickness, of the neighbouring folk, it has fairly stood the wear and tear of time, and the hand of desecrating man. Stories are told in books of its once having had a granite figure of a saint standing on its roof, of its having been thrown down and carried off; of a chapel standing near the well about the latter part of the last century, and of its font being removed by a mason near, who used it for making mortar or limewash in. The oldest country people can give me no confirmation of this.

It retains its repute, and is resorted to on Holy Thursday and the two following Thursdays, before sunrise, for the cure of eye diseases, in children chiefly, but not exclusively, and, the neighbours tell me, with great benefit. The favour of the tutelary saint is first bespoken by the offering of a pin, sometimes bent before being thrown into the water.[1]

Carew reports this of another well at Roche, not gifted with any saintly tutelage, but having some mysterious sympathy with the sea, following its ebb and flow.

I could not for a time find this second well, nor any tradition of it, but suspected that it was a remarkable instance of those basins connected by antiquaries of a just past generation with Druids, their sacrifices or lustrations. On a recent visit, however, in conversation with the villagers, I found what I had several times been in search of.

A mile and a half to the south of Roche Holy Well rises from a wide, wide moorland the three spiked bosses of Roche Rock, conspicuous against the sky for a long distance round. The central of these upthrust bosses of schorl is crowned by a once well built hermit chapelry, now in ruins. It is quite deserted now, except by summer pleasure-

[1] See Gilbert's *Hist. and Topog. Survey of Cornwall*, viii, p. 863.

seekers in the day-time, and by night haunted by spirits of the most demoniac sort, flying from some master fiend and his impossible tasks of lading out Dosmery pool with a limpet shell, or trussing the sands of the north coast with bands of the same material. The howls of the great spirit Tregeagle begging shelter at Roche and surcease from his endless tasks are among the weirdest sounds of the Cornish hills and moors.

Carew says of Roche 'that near the foot of it lieth a rock nearly level with the ground above and hollow downwards, with a winding depth which contains water reported by some of the neighbours to ebb and flow with the sea'. Of this, as of another Cornish wonder, he writes thus:—

'You neighbour-scorners, holy proud,
Goe people Roche's cell,
Farre from the World, neere to the heauens,
There, Hermits, may you dwell.
Is't true that Spring in rock hereby,
Doth tide-wise ebbe and flow?
Or have we fooles with lyers met?
Fame says it; be it so.'

Hals, writing somewhere about the early part of the seventeenth century, informs us that these rock saints, whose lives must have approached in asceticism that of S. Simeon Stylites, had disappeared, and the hermitage was some time after occupied by a solitary leper, name unknown, who, wishing to avoid infecting others with his grievous leprosy, spent the rest of his days on this pillar-rock and its chapel-crested summit. His daily wants were ministered to by his devoted daughter Gunett, or Gundred, who took daily water from a little basin for his use, not far from the rock.

This receptacle for water contained, on my last visit, but a scant supply, being only seven inches in diameter and about a foot in depth; a perfect *cul-de-sac*. As far as I could gather, it had lost the name of St. Gundred."—T. Q. C.

These two wells at Roche have often been confused, and the devoted daughter of the leper has been credited by many with the fetching of water daily from the holy well first spoken of above, instead of from the rock basin near her father's solitary home. According to Whitaker, who seems to have gained his facts as nearly as possible in every case from the fountain-head, the holy well received its sanctity from St. Conan, who was assuredly the original hermit of Roche Rock, although his name has been almost entirely lost in the descriptive title usually given to him of St. Roche, or the Holy Man of the Rock. He was one of the first bishops of Cornwall, but a hermit before a bishop; and as such was wont to retire to his rock from his house at Trefrank, on which estate his well stands, for a stricter sequestration, and a more severe solitude, during the season of Lent.

The building over the spring is in fairly good

preservation, and the water is used daily by the cottagers near by. At the bottom may be seen many bent pins, which go to prove that this well is still resorted to as a wishing-well; and inquiries elicited the information that Holy Thursday is still the favoured day for these trials of divination.

ST. RUAN'S WELL.

Whitaker, in his *Cathedral of Cornwall*, gives the following account of St. Rumon and his hermitage: "Rumon appears to have been one of the many saints who came over from Ireland into Cornwall in order to court that holy solitude, and to enjoy that heavenly contemplation in *our* vallies, and upon *our* shores, to which they had solemnly devoted their lives, and from which they were apprehensive of being drawn away, by the solicitations of their friends near them. . . .

"The scene of Rumon's retirement is fixed by his biographer in terms that indicate the latter to have written when his names were well known in the county. '*The Nemæan* wood in Cornwall,' he observes, 'was formerly very full of wild beasts; *Saint Rumon made an oratory for himself in the Nemæan wood*' (Leland).

"But where was this wood, so similarly denominated with one in ancient Arcadia? It was not, like that, in the bosom of the peninsula. It was not in the Arcadian park of Cornwall at all. It was on the exposed and beaten prominence that shoots out into the Lizard. . . .

"We find two parishes dedicated to St. Rumon at present. These are Ruan Major and Ruan

Minor, one formerly included in the other, but both included once in St. Kevern, both including also St. Grade and Landewednack once. . . .

" For the church of Grade still tithes all the estates in St. Kevern, which run from the village of Gwentor to the borders of Ruan parishes westward; tithes equally one-third of the barton of Erisey, and of the tenement of Trenoon, though at a considerable distance from it, though actually far within the parish of Ruan Major; and also tithes the tenement of Voge, though contiguous to the old glebe of Landewednack. The reason for all this pre-eminence in St. Grade, this sort of seignorial royalty in that parish over the neighbouring parishes, results from one simple circumstance, which is closely connected with my subject.

" Near the church of St. Grade is an estate, which is *known from tradition to have been the particular residence of St. Rumon*, and is therefore denominated St. Ruan at present. And as the parish of Ruan Minor is merely a narrow *lingula* of land, between St. Grade's tenements on the opposing sides of St. Kevern and of Ruan Major parishes; so are both the Ruans, Major and Minor, denominated expressly 'the church of St. Rumon' in the *Valor* of Pope Nicholas.

" Here then, though all traces of the name have now vanished, was the Nemæan wood of Cornwall. . . . Here, therefore, was the oratory of St. Rumon. . . .

"Here, near to the site of St. Grade's church, at the village still denominated St. Ruan from the fact, towards the southern extremity of the whole, and upon the leeward or eastern side of it, in a position much nearer to the sun than any other region of Britain, and as so sheltered by the woods to windward, very much warmer, did St. Rumon live; having a cell for habitation, and a chapel for his devotion. . . .

"Even the particular position of his chapel and his cell seems to be pointed out to us by the general appellation of his forest. When we find the same sort of appellation occurring in other regions of the Celtic language, we know our own to be equally Celtic with theirs. When we find the fountain of *Nemansus* in the south of France, giving name to the town of Nemansus, or Nismes, there; a river in another part of France discharging itself mediately into the Moselle, under the title of Nemera, or Nyms; and a fountain of Spain, bearing in Martial the very title of our Cornish forest, Nemea;—we see our title, like that of Nismes, derived solely from a fountain. Then we irresistibly refer this fountain to the hermitage of St. Rumon, sensible, from all we have previously learnt, of the attractiveness of a fountain to a hermit, and of a hermit's settlement being always at a fountain. And we accordingly see these circumstances combining with each other, with the notices which I have given before, and with one or two which I shall give immediately hereafter, in the present case.

"About a quarter of a mile to the north-east of Grade Church is a noted well, from which is fetched all the water used in baptism at the church. It has also a saint and a hermit belonging to it, being denominated St. Grade's Well; this 'Sancta

St. Ruan's Well.

Grada, alias Grade,' settling at it in some later period, when the parishes of Ruan Major and Minor had been both laid out in one, so superseding the name of Rumon at it, and even occasioning a new parish to be formed out of fragments of both, with Landewednack as a chapelry afterwards to it, now equally a parish church itself. But it proves its own relationship to St. Rumon by lying *very near* to *St. Ruan village*, close on the left of the road, at the head of a little hill, and facing the village. It is walled up at the back and sides with dense black iron stones; but the front, and particularly the arched entrance, is composed of coarse granite.

"The water is very fine and pellucid, exactly answering therefore to Ansonius's description of the fountain at Nismes. The water, too, which is always up to the brim of the basin, is remarkably cold in summer. . . . So faithfully represented do we discern the Nemansus and the Nemea of the continent, in the Nemea of our own Cornwall! And so judiciously had our St. Rumon selected the waters of this fountain for his own beverage! His hermitage, however, was not immediately upon the brink of it, but in what is now the village, pleasantly situated upon a little hill, like the well, and distant about a stone's throw, or rather more, from it. The village consists only of about half a dozen houses, all mean, except one on the right hand, just as you ascend the hill. This has a ruinous fence before it, denominated the court wall, and built with iron stones, enormously large.

"Here, then, we have the very hermitage of St. Rumon, afterwards converted into a chapel, like St. Mawe's; but latterly, though built of materials so strong and so massy, sinking under the weight of its own antiquity, and crumbling into ruins.

"Here, however, St. Rumon must have been

taken with that holy kind of violence which *we*, in the predominance of worldly wisdom, are apt to consider as merely ceremonial . . . in order to be made a bishop. . . . But he soon probably returned from his palace at St. German's, and resettled in his hermitage at St. Ruan. . . . He certainly died at his cell, was buried in his oratory, and then became sainted by the reverence of the country adjoining. His oratory thus expanded into a church at some distance, his wood was formed into a parish, and the wild beasts were dislodged to make room for human inhabitants. Yet his relics were preserved with religious attention at his own hermitage chapel, and his name was affixed with royal veneration to it. The place took the name of St. Ruan, as the parish church took the equal appellation of Ruan. But when 'Ordulph, duke of *Cornwall*' and Devonshire, under the Saxon sovereign, in 961, erected a monastery at Tavistock, he was so struck with their reverence for Rumon's name, Rumon's relics, and Rumon's memory, that he took up the bones of the saint and transferred them to his new monastery."—*Whitaker*.

The well has been altered by "restoration," but its former venerable and picturesque condition has been well preserved, as may be seen by the illustration. Externally it was much like the Helstone Holy Well.

The present building, which has a large niche at the back, is in good condition; there is a never-failing supply of most beautiful water, which is extraordinarily cold in summer. A few crooked pins are to be seen at the bottom, but it is not in great repute as a wishing-well, and its water is never now used for baptismal purposes. It is situated in a field beside the road, with the church path running by its door.

In the parishes of Ruan and Grade are several interesting wells. One is Park in Venton Well, at the bottom of the hill on the way to Grade Church from Cadgwith; another, not far from Grade Church, is very much in appearance like the one at Kenwyn, only this one has a curious roughly made covering of large blocks of granite leaning against each other. Whether or no they have been of more importance in the past than they are in the present we cannot tell, as no mention is anywhere made of them.

SAINT'S WELL, POLPERRO.

"In the parish of Lansallos, near Polperro, is a spring, never dry. It is much credited for its special virtues by the country folk. This reputation has long survived the edifice, which once, I believe, enclosed its holy water; and the name of the saint, its particular patron, is lost for ever. It most probably was St. Peter, the special guardian of fishermen, as on Landaviddy estate, where the well is situated, are—as little distinguishable—the faint ruins and marks of the area of the chapel of St. Peter of Porthpyre, mentioned in Bishop Brantynham's Register as existing in the year 1392.

The spring is still resorted to by those afflicted by bad eyes and other ailments, and, if 'ceremonies due are done aright,' with well-attested benefits. It must be visited on three mornings following before sunrise, fasting—a veritable injunction and rite no doubt, as witnesseth Chaucer's *Pardoner* :—

'If that the goodeman that the beest oweth
Wol every wike, er that the cōk him croweth,
Fastynge, drynke of this well a draught,
As thilke holy Jew our eldres taught,
His beestes and his stoor schal multiplie'."

—T. Q. C.

The well is still known by the name of Saint's Well among the inhabitants of Polperro; but, whatever may have been its appearance at the time the above account was written—and undoubtedly it was then unguarded by any masonry—it is now a shallow well at which cattle drink, and has but an ordinary curbstone before it.

ST. SAMPSON'S WELL, SOUTHILL.

Situated in a pretty little spot on the rectory grounds at Southill is an ancient holy well, known as St. Sampson's; it is in a very dilapidated condition; only the walls at the back and sides remain, and these are in a very ruinous state. A large ash tree grows picturesquely over what is left of the little building, one part of the root stretching across the top. No arched or shaped stones remain. The well itself is filled in now, and the stream conducted to another spot close by.

There are no traditions to be heard of in connection with this well, nor reports of peculiar properties belonging to the waters.

Probably it was dedicated to St. Sampson, Archbishop of York.

HOLY WELL, SANCREED.

On a part of the glebe not far from the church, and on a place called Chapel Down, is a holy well and baptistery. It was found by the present vicar, in 1879, covered with brambles, and has since then been carefully preserved by him.

The well is approached by steps which lead down to it. No carved stones are to be seen in the building, and no traditions could be gleaned from the old man who guided us to it. The chapel stands at the back of the well on higher ground; no authentic history of it can be found, so probabiy the little building was only used as a baptistery in connection with the holy well.

SCARLET'S WELL, BODMIN.

"Of the Bodmin holy wells Scarlet's Well, the most renowned of them, is in a valley threaded by a brooklet which, issuing from the grounds of the priory, welling in its well-stocked ponds, runs through the town of Bodmin to pay its tribute to the Camel river at Dunmeer. It was once more secluded, a footpath only leading that way; now the Bodmin and Wadebridge railway runs a few feet from it. Consequently the Naiad has gone; and the virtues of the limpid streamlet, which runs as freely as of old, have left it for ever, except in the memory of a very few and very old devotees, by whom a morning's walk for a drink or an eye bath is found to be repaid by never-failing cure. There are no marks of building, but the shape of the excavation leads me to suppose that the water was once enclosed in an edifice. There are two separate issues: one which simply oozes, and another, a considerable and constant stream, which rises from a considerable depth. Carew, in his *Survey of Cornwall,* thus speaks of it:—

'Within short space after the great fame dispersed touching the rare effects of Warwickshire wells, some idle envious head raised a bruit that there rested no less virtue, forsooth, for healing all diseases, in a plentiful spring near unto Bodmin, called Scarlet's Well; which report grew so far and so fast that folk ran flocking thither in huge numbers from all quarters. But the neighbour justices, finding the abuse, and looking into the consequence, forbad the resort, sequestered the spring, and suppressed the miracle. Howbeit, the water should seem to be healthful if not helpful; for it retaineth this extraordinary quality, that the same is weightier than the ordinary of his kind, and will continue the best part of a year without alteration of scent or taste; only you shall see it represent many colours like the rainbow, which (in my conceit) argueth a running through some mineral vein, and therewithal a possessing of some virtue.'

Testing the accuracy of Carew's statement respecting the remarkable weight of this water, I have on many occasions, and at various seasons of the year, kept records of the stream, and have found its temperature at midsummer and Christmas, in hot sunshine, and hard frost alike, at 53° Fahrenheit; and its specific gravity generally that of distilled water. On one visit only, and that after heavy thunderstorms and floods of rain, did I find it 1·005. This was caused probably by surface soilure. It will thus be seen that Carew was misinformed as to the qualities of the water."—T. Q. C.

Maclean, in his *History of Trigg Minor*, writes that "this well probably derived its name from a family called Scarlet, anciently inhabitants of this town". A certain John Scarlet was M.P. for Bodmin in 1312.

TREGAMINION CHAPEL WELL, MORVAH.

This well, which is about four feet square and three feet deep, lies in the corner of a field on Tregaminion farm, and is now entirely without building or protection of any kind. Near this well, in former days, stood a chapel in the same field; but no trace of this building now remains. The water is never used, but in years gone by it is said to have possessed most extraordinary healing qualities, and to have performed many miraculous cures. Few persons remember its ancient reputation, though there may be some lingering recognition of its sanctity in the fact that the corner of the field in which the well is situated is never tilled; indeed, except for the occasional visit of an antiquarian, the spot is rarely disturbed.

ST. WARNA'S WELL, SCILLY ISLES.

Respecting this ancient well, one cannot do better than describe its gradual neglect in the words of Miss Courtney: "St. Warna, who presided over wrecks, was the patron saint of St. Agnes, another of the principal islands. She crossed over here from Ireland in a wicker boat covered with hides, and landed at St. Warna's Bay. Like many other saints she had her holy well; and often the superstitious inhabitants of St. Agnes (five families in all), who enjoyed the reputation of being the most daring and unscrupulous amongst the Scilly wreckers of those days, threw crooked pins into it, and daily invoked and prayed her to send them 'a rich wreck'. . . .

"From that time St. Warna's Well was neglected; there was no one left the day after the twelfth day, as had been the custom, to clean it out and return her thanks for her bounty: it gradually got filled with stones, and at the present day is little more than a hole." [1]

[1] *Cornish Feasts and Folk-lore*, Miss M. A. Courtney.

ST. WENNA'S WELL, ST. WENN.

In the parish of St. Wenn there was, according to the *Parochial History of Cornwall*, a holy well dedicated to St. Wenna, grand-daughter of Brechan, King of Wales. The Rev. W. S. Lach-Szyrma writes of this saint: "She was martyred by the Saxon heathens in Wales, but probably lived in St. Wenn parish and consecrated it to God's service". The water of this well was at one time used for baptismal purposes; but that must have been very many years ago, for the inhabitants of St. Wenn village, both old and young, in answer to inquiries, declared that they had never even heard of the well; there appeared to be neither trace nor recollection of it remaining.

HOLY WELL, ZENNOR.

There was at one time a holy well in the parish of Zennor, situated on that isthmus which connects the Gurnard's Head with the mainland; a chapel stood near by, but it is not known by whom the buildings were sanctified, nor to whom dedicated.

Dotted here and there on dangerous parts of the coast some saint or other seems to have formerly built a chapel, and had a consecrated well or baptistery attached—at Constantine, St. Leven, and St. Loy—but time and storms have almost effaced them all. Of the well at Zennor there is now nothing remaining.